OFF THE DOLE

Brian Johnston

ISBN-979850931760

Cover design by: Art Painter
Library of Congress Control Number: 2018675309
Printed in the United States of America

This book is dedicated to the men and women of Newfoundland that served in both world wars, especially to those that served in the Merchant Marine and Forestry Service that had to wait for so many years before they were properly reconized and compensated for their service.

The Battle of the Atlantic was not won by any navy or air force. It was won by the courage, fortitude and determination of the British and Allied Merchant Navy.

REAR ADMIRAL LEONARD MURRAY, COMMANDER-
IN-CHIEF, CANADIAN NORTH ATLANTIC.

CONTENTS

PREFACE

The residents of Harbour Breton are in the depths of the Great Depression. People are struggling to feed and clothe themselves and their families. Suddenly in 1940, Newfoundland and the rest of the world, are plunged into another world war. This book is a story of the depression and war years told through the lives of fishing captain, Bill Johnston, Dr. Albert Lewis and their families.

CHAPTER 1

"Hide them rabbits under your jacket, Joe. We don't want that old bastard, John Brown, seeing them and cutting off our dole," said Lawrence Johnston to his friend Joe Hickey.

"Yes, that son of a bitch saw Tom Skinner the other day with a brace of rabbits and cut off his and his poor mother's dole for the month," replied Joe as the two young men continued down a path from the hillside that led to Lawrence's house. It was a beautiful spring day in the fishing community of Harbour Breton and the two young men were just returning from an early morning trip to check snares that they had set just the day before.

The year was 1939 and the people of Harbour Breton and the rest of Newfoundland were still suffering in the depths of the Great Depression. Things had been extremely hard for the people of the island of Newfoundland since the end of the First World War in 1918. The government of the island had incurred a huge war debt as a result of supporting the Newfoundland Regiment during its' time overseas. The government struggled to pay this huge debt after the end of the war. The economy of the island had suffered as well, shortly after 1918. The foreign markets of the world had been glutted with salt cod and as a result the price for fish worldwide had been cut by half. All this, along with the crash of the stock market in 1929, had devastated the economy of the island. There was also less demand for commodities that were produced in Newfoundland, such as dried cod, iron ore and wood pulp and paper. All these factors had led to wide scale unemployment and poverty. The country of Newfoundland was near bankruptcy trying to cover the war debt along with trying to support its poor and unemployed, starving people. Things had become so bleak that there had been riots in St. John's in 1932 against the Prime Minister of the time, Richard Squires. As a result of all these combined problems, Newfoundland relinquished its nationhood and reverted to a Commission Government controlled by Great Britain.

Many people of the island were now dependent on a government support program that had been given the name of "The Dole" by the people of the island. Each unemployed single person received a monthly allotment which included 25lbs of flour, 4lbs of salt pork, 2lbs of beans, 1lb of split peas, 3/4lbs of cocoa and one quart of molasses. People in St. John's received a ration of vegetables as well, but those living in rural Newfoundland were expected to grow their own vegetables. This allotment did not meet the nutritional requirements for one person for a month and as a result there was widespread malnutrition, disease and an increase in the infant mortality rate.

Lawrence and Joe walked into the home of Lawrence's parents, Bill and Martha Johnston. Lawrence's mother, Martha, was sitting at the kitchen table feeding her newborn baby, Kyran. She looked toward the two young men and said, "What have you two been up to? By the looks on your faces I can tell it's been no good."

Joe unbuttoned his jacket, pulled out two skinned rabbits, looked at Martha and smiled.

"Did anyone see you with them rabbits?" asked Martha.

"No, Mrs. Johnston, we hid them good. We didn't want that old bastard, John Brown, seeing us," replied Joe.

"Now, you watch your language young man, or I'll tell your mother and she'll wash your mouth out with soap," said Martha as she got up from her chair and put the baby into a crib.

Just then the door opened and Lawrence's 18-year-old sister, Angie, walked into the room holding the hands of her two young brothers, Fred and Gerald.

Martha looked at Angie and said, "Angie take one of them rabbits and hide it in a pot in the back kitchen. I'll cook it for our supper - your father loves a bit of rabbit soup."

"Yes, Mom," replied Angie as she released her young brother's hands and told them to go sit down on the day bed.

Angie took one of the rabbits from Joe and left the room to do as her mother had instructed.

Martha then looked at Joe and said, "You better get home now and take that other rabbit home to your mother. Make sure you hides it good, and no one sees it. That's all your poor mother needs now is for someone to see that."

Joe put the other rabbit inside his jacket and then buttoned it up. He looked at Lawrence and said, "I'll see you after dinner." Joe then left to go back to his home.

John Brown was the government agent for Harbour Breton and the surrounding communities. It was his job to distribute the monthly government allotments for each person and to make sure that no one was working and still collecting the dole. Any person that worked and received any money at all, had to report it to the agent. Even if someone had something as simple as rabbits that they had hunted, they could lose a portion of their monthly allotment. John Brown was a hard man who seemed to take great enjoyment in the control he had over the people of the community.

Martha looked at Lawrence and said, "You go get washed up now and then go out and help your brothers. They should be home soon with the wood. Your father should be home for his dinner in a bit. Thank God Jake is taking out the other schooner this year and we can get off that dole."

Things had been extremely hard this past year for the Johnston family as well as most of the other families of Harbour Breton. There had been very few boats fishing these past years because of the decline in price and demand for dried cod. Over the past several years there had been a dramatic increase in the number of trawlers fishing the waters of the Grand Banks. These motorized steel vessels put their catches on ice instead of salting and drying it. There was a much higher demand for fresh frozen fish over the salted and dried version. Most men only fished now to feed themselves and their families. Jake Smith had tied up all but one of his inshore fishing boats. He had also sold one of his schooners a couple of years ago to help keep his business out of bankruptcy. Last year, Jake had made the decision not to send his remaining schooner out to the fishing grounds as well.

Bill Johnston was grateful that he was chosen to captain the schooner, Sally Smith, because it allowed him to make enough money to keep his family fed. Last year, that changed when Jake had decided it was not feasible for him to run even one schooner. Bill had spent the previous year receiving dole payments like many other families of the community. They had struggled to make ends meet and keep themselves fed. Bill and his family were very thankful that they had a bountiful garden last year. Bill and Martha had managed to save a bit of money during the good years, but they had to use up almost all their money before they were eligible for government assistance. Bill and Martha had a large family. Bill's daughters, Marg and Liz now lived in Corner Brook with families of their own. Bill and Martha had one daughter, Angie, and seven sons ranging in age from four months old to 15 years of age - Felix, Leo, Bill, Lawrence, Fred, Gerald and Kyran, who was the baby.

Bill Johnston was taking a quick look around the schooner to make sure everything was in order before he would head home for his dinner. The previous year had been a long, hard one for Bill. It had been the first time in his adult life that he had not been able to fish and make a living for his family. He would be captain of the schooner, Sally Smith, and

Art Hunt would be sailing as his mate this spring. There had been many men eager to sign on for the fishing season, but Bill and Jake had been able to only select a few of the men that wanted a chance to work. Bill had hoped to get a couple of his older sons on with him as dorymen. He realized that this would not be possible when Jake had told him that he wanted to make sure that only one man per family was working on the schooner. Jake wanted to give as many families as possible, a chance at making a living and getting off the dole this year.

Many of their crew from years past had moved out of Newfoundland to try and find work in other places. Dick Snook had moved to Gloucester with his wife, Mary, and their children four years ago. He had been lucky enough to get a berth on a steel fishing trawler as a deck hand. Bill had been talking with Dick's brother-in-law, Dr. Albert Lewis, a few days ago. Albert had received a letter from his sister, Mary. She had written that Dick would be going mate on the trawler this spring. Bill had no doubts that Dick would be captain of one of those trawlers sometime in the next few years.

Bill's old friend and mentor, Captain John Lewis, had passed away five years ago and John's beloved wife, Maggie, the year before. The only member of the Lewis family left living in Harbour Breton now was Dr. Albert Lewis. John's daughter, Liza, along with her husband and family had moved on as well following the death of her father.

Dr. Albert Lewis now oversaw the day-to-day operations of the new Harbour Breton Cottage Hospital that had been built in 1936. There was one other doctor on staff. There were also four full-time nurses and a few local people employed as support staff. Things had been terribly busy at the hospital since it had opened. This was mainly due to the hard times that were being experienced in the community. There were a variety of diseases running rampant now such as beriberi and tuberculosis. These diseases along with many others, had resulted in a high infant mortality rate in the community. All these factors were a direct result of peoples' inability to buy the basic food items that were needed for their survival. The meager rations issued by the government were barely enough to keep people alive. Things were so bad that there had recently been several deaths in the Fortune Bay area that had been attributed to malnutrition. People did not have any money to buy clothes for themselves or their children, so many parents were not sending their children to school. Most people of the area were not able to pay for any medical expenses, as well. Residents of the community were not visiting the hospital when they were ill because of their inability to pay. Dr. Lewis did what he could to help the people that could not afford to pay for his services. He had soon come to realize though, that there was only so much that he himself could do.

"George, do we have all the grub aboard?" asked Bill.

George Parrott, the cook, shook his head and said, "Yes, Skipper b'y, the little bit that we got. There's not much that came aboard. We'll be eating lots of fish this trip - not too much of anything else came. We got lots of potatoes and vegetables, anyway."

"Yes, George b'y, we'll have to make do with what we got. Nobody's going to starve as long as we get some fish. It's hard times everywhere - Jake sent aboard what he could. We're lucky he's sending the boat out at all this year," replied Bill.

"Yes, Skipper b'y, you're right about that. I'll make do with whatever we got. I'm happy we can get off that goddam dole this year," said George.

"How is Olive and the youngsters doing?" asked Bill.

"It's been a hard year, Skipper. We was worried we wouldn't be able to send Theresa and Sam to school this year." replied George.

"Yes, it's been hard times for everyone. I guess I better head home for dinner. Do you have anything for yourself to eat, George? You can come home and have some dinner with us if you wants," Bill asked this as George was the only crewman that did not live in Harbour Breton.

"Thank you for the offer, Skipper b'y. I got a bit of dried fish and potato for my dinner." replied George.

"Ok then. If you see Art, tell him I might be a bit late getting back. I have to go and talk with Jake after dinner," said Bill.

"Ok, Skipper b'y, see you after dinner."

Bill had just finished his dinner; he walked outside and went over to where his sons, Lawrence and Bill, were sawing up wood and stacking it in a pile to allow the wood to dry over the summer months.

"How are you making out boy's? Where's Felix and Leo?" asked Bill.

"They're gone back in over the hill to cut some more wood," replied Bill Jr.

"What time is you leaving to go fishing?" asked Lawrence.

"We should be leaving in the morning," replied Captain Johnston.

"It's too bad we couldn't get a chance to go fishing with ya this year," said Lawrence.

"Maybe next year I'll be able to take one of you boys with me. Maybe things will pick up next year and a few more schooners will get back out fishing. I'm just happy that I can fish again this year. I better head back down aboard the schooner - you fellers finish sawing up the rest of the wood and then go get some water for your mother. I'll see you boys tonight," said Captain Johnston.

"Ok, Dad," replied the boys.

◆ ◆ ◆

Captain Bill Johnston walked the well-trodden dirt path that led from his home to the dock where the schooners were tied up. Jake Smith's store and the old Newman Plantation were also located in this area of town. Along the way, he stopped to talk with several members of the community to discuss the weather and how the preparations for the start of a new fishing season were going. Bill arrived at his destination and walked up the wooden stairs that led to Jake Smith's store. Bill walked inside the store and looked around. He saw Jake standing at the counter talking with the government agent, John Brown. Bill could see that the men seemed to be arguing about something, so he stood back and waited for the two men to finish their conversation.

"Damn it, John! You mean you want me to cut off that poor family's dole for the month? They're all half starving as it is. That poor woman lost her husband last year and she's trying to raise five youngsters on her own. She already had one of her little boys die a few months ago. They don't know for sure why, but the poor little thing was probably half-starved," said Jake.

"I don't make the rules, Mr. Smith, I just follow them. I saw her oldest boy with a brace of rabbits yesterday. The rules are the rules. I don't want to lose my job" replied John Brown.

"Who in the name of God would have said anything. You got no heart at all, my son. You could have turned a blind eye to it or just have given the boy a warning. You know just as well as everyone else how hard things have been for that poor woman since she lost her husband," said Jake.

"Rules are rules and that's the end of it. I'm not going to argue about it anymore. If you don't want to distribute the dole rations anymore, I'm sure that one of the other merchants in the harbour will take over," said John Brown as he looked at Jake and smiled that crooked, hateful grin that he was so known for.

Jake just lowered his head. He knew there was no sense in arguing with the man. His mind was made up and there was no changing it now.

John Brown was the most hated man in Harbour Breton. He had arrived in the community last year to take over the job of government agent. The agent was the person employed by the government to oversee the distribution of the assistance program. John Brown had arrived in Harbour Breton from St. John's. He was not a native Newfoundlander but had moved to the island seven years ago from England. He was 30 years of age and stood five feet two inches tall. He was a very portly man who was bald with a crooked, flat nose and several missing teeth. The people of the town had wondered how he could be so big while the rest of the island was starving. They all knew full well that he survived on a lot more than the monthly ration that was issued to every-one else. John Brown took great joy in throwing his weight around and holding the lives of the people of the community in his hands. Jake knew why he was doing what he was doing to the poor Skinner woman. John Brown was not beyond trying to offer special treatment or extra rations to young women in exchange for sexual favours. He had tried this with the poor widow Skinner, and she had spurned his advances. Jake knew full well that now she and her poor young children would suffer for it.

John Brown smiled, nodded and tipped his hat to Jake. Then he turned and headed out the door.

 Bill walked over to where Jake was standing and said, "I hate that son of a bitch. I wanted to grab him by the back of the neck and put my boot up his arse."

"I know Bill b'y, but what can I say to the man? This bit of government business that we are getting is the only thing keeping us afloat and he knows that. I'll try and help the poor Skinner family as much as I can. I can't afford to give out credit to anyone any-more, not even the people that I know can pay me back," said Jake as he shook his head.

The men were silent for a moment and then Jake asked, "So, Bill, are you fellers all ready to sail to-morrow?"

"Yes sir, Jake b'y, we're all ready to go. Hopefully, we'll be able to get a few fish," replied Bill.

"Catching the fish is not the problem, Bill - it's trying

to sell it that's going to give me the trouble. There's not much of a market for the dried fish anymore. All they want in the states now is frozen fish," said Jake.

"Hopefully, things will start to pick up this year," said Bill

"I'm sorry that I couldn't send down more pork, beef and flour but that's all I could afford," said Jake.

"Now, don't you go worrying about that, Jake. Nobody is going to starve as long as we have some fish and potatoes. We is all happy to be back at the fish this year and get off the damn dole," replied Bill.

Jake smiled and said, "Hopefully everything will change this year. I was reading in the paper that things in the states were starting to improve a bit so hopefully this depression will end soon."

"I guess I better get back down aboard the boat," said Bill.

"Ok Bill, I'll be down in the morning to see you fellers off," said Jake

"Hopefully, we'll get a bit of good luck this year. God knows it's about time we got some," said Bill.

Both men shook hands and then Bill turned and headed out the door. As Bill walked out of the store, several women walked in.

"Good morning, ladies. What can I do for you this morning?" asked Jake as he walked over to where the women were standing.

CHAPTER 2

Albert Lewis was in his office at the Harbour Breton Cottage Hospital. He was sitting behind a large oak desk. The walls of the room were a milky white and the floor was covered with a pale blue linoleum that glistened with a coat of fresh wax. The room had several large bookcases that contained a variety of medical books. There was a large window behind the desk that let in the light of the midday sun. The door opened and a nurse entered the room - she motioned for a woman and her young son to come in. Albert looked up from a book that he was reading and said, "Good day, Mrs. Augot, what can I do for you today?"

"Well, Doctor, it's not me, but my youngest boy Jack, here," the woman said as she pointed to the young boy of eight who was standing next to her.

"Well, then what seems to be the problem?" asked Dr. Lewis.

"The boy is tired all the time and he tells me his legs and arms feel funny, like they're tingling," said the young boy's mother.

Albert went over and put out his hand for the young boy to come to him. He reached down and picked the boy up and carried him over to the examination table. Albert removed the boy's shirt and thought to himself, the poor child is skin and bones - he looks like he's starving. Having to examine near-starving children had become an all-too-common practice for Albert these past few years.

"I was worried he's getting the rickets. He's been taking his cod liver oil every day so I don't know what could be going on with him." said the boy's mother.

Albert examined the boy and after a few moments he then told the child to put his shirt back on. He looked at the boy's mother and said, "Have you been using the brown flour for your cooking?"

"No, Doctor, me husband Jim hates it - he says he only likes the white flour, so we don't get it any-more," replied the woman.

"What about the Cocomalt at school? Has he been taking his regular dose every day?"

The woman paused for a moment and said, "He's not going to school this year, doctor - we got no money to send him or any of the other youngsters anymore. We can barely keep ourselves from starv-ing to death. If it weren't for me mother and father, I wouldn't have had the money to come and see you today."

"He doesn't have rickets, but he may be getting

something else called beriberi," said Albert.

"Oh my God, no! What's that?" The woman asked as tears ran down her cheeks.

"It's not serious yet but you have to start using the brown flour. Did you have any beets, cabbage and turnip greens this year in your garden?"

"Yes, doctor but the boy won't touch his vegetables," said the woman.

Albert looked at the boy and motioned for him to come over.

"Now young man, you have to start eating some of your vegetables, ok. You don't want to get sick now, do you?" asked Albert.

The boy shook his head and said, "No Doctor."

"Mrs. Augot, I want you to tell your husband that the brown flour has vitamins in it that help prevent diseases like beriberi. You tell him I said that he will have to learn to like it. That's if he doesn't want his children to get sick. I don't want to scare you, but beriberi can be serious if it goes untreated."

Albert reached into one of the drawers of his desk and pulled out a small can of Cocomalt mix and passed it to the boy's mother.

"Dr. Lewis sir, I can't pay for this," said the woman as she wiped tears from her eyes.

"You don't have to - don't worry about that. There's enough there for a couple of weeks - just give him some every day. Make sure that you start using the brown flour and the boy starts eating his vegetables. If you do everything that I've said, he'll start getting better soon. One more thing Mrs. Augot …try not to cook your vegetables for too long. If you overcook your vegetables it takes all the vitamins and nutrients out of them."

The woman started to cry again and then she said, "Thank you so much, Dr. Lewis. I don't know what this town would do without you. You're a good man."

"Now, now, Mrs. Augot that's ok. Please just remember what I said."

As Albert walked the woman and her young son to the door, he said, "If your husband gives you a hard time about the flour and how you cook your vegetables just come see me and I'll go and have a talk with him."

"I will, Dr. Lewis, and thank you again," the woman said as she left Albert's office.

The nurse looked in the door and said, "That's the last one for the day, Dr. Lewis."

"Ok Sarah, thank you. I just have a few things to do and then I'm going to head home for the day."

Albert walked into his house, removed his boots and hung his overcoat on a hook in the porch. He then opened the door and walked into the kitchen of his house. Cora, Albert's wife of 20 years, was sitting at the kitchen table talking to their house-keeper, Jane.

"Hello, Dear," said Cora as she looked up at her husband. "How was your day?"

Just then, Jane got up from the table and said, "I better get back to work, Mrs. Lewis. I have to get the clothes in off the line - it looks like it might rain."

The young woman got up from the table and headed out the door to go about her work. Albert went to the kitchen table, pulled out a chair and sat down next to his wife. Cora looked at her husband and thought to herself how tired he looked. These last few years had taken a toll on Albert. He had to deal with all these new illnesses that were being caused by malnutrition. Albert tried to help as many of the community members as he could, that could not afford to pay for a hospital visit. Cora had finally convinced her husband that there was only so much he could do and if he kept trying to see so many people outside his regular working hours, he was going to get run down and sick himself.

"My day was good dear and how about you?" replied Albert.

Albert and Cora had been married now for 20 years. They had three children. A son, John, who was 19 years old and away in St. John's studying at Memorial University College. He was just about to finish his second year of studies in preparation to continue to medical school in England and follow in his father's footsteps. Albert and Cora had two young daughters as well who were 15 and 16. Both young girls were away for their first year of studies at The Bishop Spencer School for Girls in St. John's. It had been a shock for Albert and Cora to have all their children leave the nest within the past two years. Cora had decided that she would start teaching again this year. She had told her husband that she needed to have something to keep her occupied now that their children were all away at school. Cora had stopped teaching not long after the birth of their second child.

"I had a good day, Dear. I spent most of it chatting with Jane. She's a bright young woman and seems genuinely nice, as well. What about you, Albert dear? You look tired."

"It's been a long day...so many sick children. If this damn depression doesn't end soon, there'll be more death and sickness than this island can handle," replied Albert.

Cora got up from her chair went over to her husband, wrapped her arms around him and gave him a kiss.

"Now that always makes me feel better," said Albert as his hand slipped down his wife's back. He put his hand on her bottom and gave it a slight squeeze.

"Now, Dr. Lewis, you better behave yourself...young

Jane will be back in with the clothes soon."

Albert smiled and gave his wife a kiss and said, "We can finish what you started tonight. How are things going with school, my love?"

Cora looked at her husband, shook her head smiled and said, "It was good, I guess. There are even fewer children attending school this year. Poor people can't afford to feed and clothe their children let alone send them to school."

They both paused for a moment and then Cora said, "Let's go into the parlor and have a brandy before supper."

Just then the door opened and the young house-keeper, Jane, walked inside. She had just started working with Albert and Cora a few weeks ago. They had decided to hire someone to cook and clean the house so that Cora could concentrate on getting back to the work of teaching. Jane was 18 years old and from the nearby community of Boxy. She was a tall, dark-haired young woman who had caught the eye of many of the young single men of the community.

Jane put down her clothes basket and said, "There's some mail here for you, Mrs. Lewis."

Cora walked over to where the young woman was standing, took the mail and said, "Thank you, Jane - we're going into the parlor."

"Ok Mrs. Lewis, I'm going to put these clothes away

and then I'll start supper."

"Ok, Jane, thank you," said Cora as she and Albert left the room, walked into the parlor and sat in their chairs near the fireplace. Cora got up from her chair, walked over to the window and opened the curtains to let in the light of the setting sun.

"Here's your paper from St. Johns," said Cora as she handed Albert the newspaper and started to look through the rest of their mail.

"We have a letter from John," she said as she laid down the rest of the mail and proceeded to open the letter and read it to herself. Albert started to read his newspaper.

"I guess that John will be home for a visit over Easter. He must have changed his mind. I'm sure he said that he wouldn't be home this year. I wonder why he changed his mind."

"Well, that's nice. It will be good to see him," replied Albert.

Cora got up from her chair, went over to the cabinet and took out a couple of glasses then proceeded to pour a glass of brandy for each of them. As she walked over and held out the glass for her husband, he did not look up from his paper. She could see that there was a deep look of concern on his face as he intently read his newspaper.

"Here you are, Dear," said Cora as she held out the glass of brandy.

"Oh, sorry Dear, I didn't see you," replied Albert as he took the glass from his wife's hand.

"What are you reading about? I can tell by the look on your face it's not good news," said Cora.

Albert paused for a moment, took a sip of his brandy and laid the glass on the side table that was between their chairs. "Oh, its Europe. It looks like Hitler and Stalin have signed some sort of nonaggression pact. I fear there's going to be another war in Europe soon. The Germans have already moved into Austria and Czechoslovakia. I can't believe this may all be happening again. You think they would have learned a lesson from that first damn war."

Albert put down the paper and took another sip of his brandy. Cora did not say anything for a moment and then she said, "Maybe cooler heads will prevail, and people will come to their senses."

"I somehow doubt that very much, but I certainly hope they do. That Hitler is a fascist fanatic, I think. The French have a powerful Army and Navy now so hopefully the Germans will not be stupid enough to start another war. Anyway, that's enough talk about that. What else did John have to say in his letter?" asked Albert.

"Not much else…just that school is going well and he's looking forward to getting home for a break. He says that the girls are settling in well and that he tries to get over to see them once a week."

"Well, that's good. It'll be good to see him again. We

should try and get to St. John's to visit him and the girls this summer," said Albert.

"Yes, I was thinking that, too. It would be nice to get away for a bit," replied Cora.

"What do we have for supper, my love?"

"We're having some fresh fried salmon - Mrs. Hunt dropped some off today. She said it was the least she could do for you since you came over to see her mother and didn't charge them anything."

"That was nice of her, but we shouldn't take anything from these poor people. They have so little for themselves these days. They can barely feed themselves let alone pay for medical service," said Albert.

"It makes them feel better when they give you some little thing for your help."

"Yes, I guess you're right. Maybe some day governments will pay for everyone's medical services. They don't mind spending it on weapons of war to kill other humans. If they spent some time and effort trying to help the poor of this world, it would be a much better place."

"Well, that's enough dwelling on things I can't change. That salmon smells good - I can't wait for supper. We should try and get to bed early tonight," Albert said as he reached over and took his wife's hand, looked at her and winked.

Just then the door opened, and Jane looked inside

and said, "Supper is ready, Mr. and Mrs. Lewis."

"Thank you, Jane, we'll be right out," replied Cora as she and Albert got up from their chairs and headed to the dining room for their evening meal.

CHAPTER 3

It was another beautiful spring day. The crew of the schooner, Sally Smith, were busy preparing their boat for the upcoming trip to the fishing grounds. The wharf near Newman's old store was busier this morning than it had been it quite some time. Skipper Bill Johnston and Jake Smith were standing on the dock near the gangway of the schooner.

"Well, Bill, it looks like you fellers are going to have a good first day on the water," said Jake Smith, owner of the schooner Sally Smith.

"Yes, Jake b'y, I think so. The boys are all grateful to you for letting us get back to work this year," replied Bill.

"I got some good news yesterday. I heard back from a buyer in Grand Bank. He's going to take all our fish this year. The price is not the greatest, that's for sure so we will have to try and keep our costs down as much as we can. The wages for the men will not be too good either, I'm afraid. Most of them may only just break even this year," said Jake.

"Now Jake b'y, that's good news that you got someone to buy the fish. Don't go worrying about the wages either - anything is better than that damn dole. We'll try and keep the grub bill down as much as we can. We can eat fish three times a day like we use to when we was dory mates," laughed Bill Johnston.

"Ok Bill," laughed Jake. "I better get back and open up the store. People will be getting their food rations today so it's going to be a busy one for sure. Have a safe trip and I'll see you in a month or so I guess," said Jake.

The men shook hands then Bill turned and headed up the gangway of the schooner, Sally Smith.

"Alright Art b'y, lets get this old girl underway so we can get back out at the fish," yelled Bill as he stepped onto the well-worn deck of the schooner.

The boat had been laid up for a year, but the men had worked hard to repair what needed to be fixed. There was no money for any new rigging or equipment so they had done what they could, to get the schooner seaworthy with the limited resources that were available to them.

The Sally Smith was under full sail now and heading out of Fortune Bay into open water. There were a few other schooners underway this morning. A small plume of smoke could be seen rising from a couple of the schooners in the bay this morning.

It was becoming more and more common the past few years for schooners to be equipped with a small engine. Jake had considered installing an engine in his schooner, but the cost was more than he could afford during these hard times.

Bill was at the wheel along with his mate Art Hunt who was standing next to him. Bill looked at Art and said, "I'm glad that Jake didn't put an engine in this old girl. Them damn things are so noisy, and the stink of those fumes is enough to make you sick."

"Yes sir, Skipper b'y...I'm happy to be back on the water again. Last year was a rough one," said Art.

"Yes, Art b'y, how's your wife doing now?" asked Bill.

"Pretty good, I guess, but it's awful hard losing a baby. But you know all about that, Skipper b'y," replied Art.

Both men were silent for a moment. Art Hunt and his wife Gertie had lost their young son just six months ago. The baby had been just a few weeks old. The child had suddenly become ill with a fever and died within a few days of getting sick. Infant deaths had become all to common these past few years.

"I better go check on the boys, Skipper, and make sure everything is stowed away. I'll be back in a bit to relieve you so you can go down for a smoke and a cup of tea," said Art.

"Ok Art b'y, sounds good," said Bill as he altered his

course a bit to the southwest and took another look around. It will be nice to get back fishing again, Bill thought to himself.

The sun was just starting to rise now as the schooner, Sally Smith, arrived at the fishing grounds. It was another beautiful June morning. The seas were calm and there was hardly any swell to speak of. Bill and Art looked on as the crew went about their duties. The men lowered the sails and prepared to drop anchor.

"Well, Art b'y, we got a wonderful day to start. Let's just hope there's a few fish around," said Bill.

"Yes sir, Skipper b'y," replied Art.

"All right then, boys, let's get the anchor out and start to bait up. Time to get at 'er!" yelled Bill.

Bill, as well as all the other crewmen were happy to be back fishing. Fishing was the only way they knew to provide for themselves and their families. Even after all these years as being skipper, it felt strange for Bill not to be going out in the dory. He missed the hard work, but he was captain now, so he always needed to be aboard his boat.

It was a beautiful spring morning with a cool breeze blowing from the west. Bill had picked the spot on the Saint Pierre banks that had given both him and his late friend and mentor, John Lewis, luck these past decades. Bill had learned much from his friend, John Lewis, and it was days like these that brought back fond memories of him. Bill looked on as his dorymen rowed away. He then walked up to check the anchor cable and scanned the horizon. There were smoke plumes visible now all around them. He could see many trawlers fishing the Grand Banks. Most of these steel motorized vessels were from American ports like Gloucester. There were fewer and fewer schooners fishing the banks and even those schooners that came from the USA now, iced their catches instead of salting it. The trawlers used nets that were set directly from the boat instead of the traditional hook and line that had been used for so many years. The days of dory fishing were coming to an end. Fresh fish was a more desired product that brought a much better price on the market. Bill often wondered to himself if maybe some day these steel trawlers would sail from Newfoundland fishing communities like Harbour Breton.

The dories were coming back alongside now with their first catches of the year. As Bill looked on, he could see that most of the dories were about half full. Not as good as the catches had been in years past but he certainly had seen much worse.

"Not too bad, Skipper," yelled Art from his dory.

"Yes, Art b'y, it could be worse - we could all be still home collecting that damn dole again this year," replied Bill.

All the men laughed as they started to pitch their catches aboard and prepared to head back out for another set before dinner.

"That was a good supper, George. I loves the haddock boiled in a bit of salt beef," said Art.

"Yes sir, but it would be nice to have a bit more of the beef," said another crewman.

"Be thankful you got some beef at all. We should all count ourselves lucky Jake was able to send this boat out at all this year," Bill replied harshly.

The crew all lowered their heads and continued to eat without complaints from anyone else.

"All right boys finish up and get into bed – it's going to be an early start in the morning," yelled Art.

The sun was starting to rise, and the men had their dories in the water in preparation to start another day of fishing. Everyone was either on deck now or in the dories. Suddenly one of the crewmen yelled, "FIRE!" Bill turned around to look to where the crewmember was pointing. He could see smoke and flames coming from the galley. Bill knew they did not have much time. He yelled to his men who remained aboard, "Get in the dories!"

"Is everyone on deck? Where's George?" yelled Bill.

"I'm right here, Skipper," replied George as he ran over to where Bill was standing.

The flames and smoke were getting much worse by the second. The old schooners hull and rigging were as dry as kindling.

"In the dories, boys - make it quick!" said Bill as the last of his crew climbed off the burning schooner. Bill took one last look around and then climbed aboard a dory. As the men all rowed away, they looked back at their schooner that was now fully engulfed in flames.

The men all looked on in silence. Bill looked at George and asked, "Was there something left on the stove?"

"No, Skipper b'y, nothing - everything was all cleared away from breakfast I don't know what could have happened," replied the cook.

Bill paused for a moment and wondered to himself that maybe it was that old stove. Jake was planning on getting a new one this year but had to put it off until he sold some fish.

"Well, at least we all got off in one piece. Thank God that didn't happen in the middle of the night…we would have all been burned for sure," said Art.

"Ok, boys let's get all these dories tied together so we don't get separated," said Bill as he scanned the horizon. Bill could see that there were several other schooners and vessels in the area. He knew that the flames from their burning schooner would be visible for miles. As Bill looked to the east, he could see a trawler making its way towards them.

As the steel trawler came to a stop, the dories from the burning schooner slowly made their way alongside the trawler. It looks like a Gloucester boat, Bill thought to himself. The crewmen of the trawler lowered a rope ladder over the side so the men of the schooner could climb aboard. Bill looked up and saw a familiar face looking down at him. Bill was the last man to get aboard as he wanted to make sure that all his crew were safely aboard the schooner. Bill stepped onto the deck of the trawler as his old friend and shipmate Dick Snook came over to greet him and shake his hand.

"Well, Dick b'y, it's a good thing that you fellers showed up when you did," said Bill.

"Yes, Bill, good to see you. I'm happy that we were close enough to help. We were just about to get underway for Gloucester. We're all loaded and ready to head back. What happened, Bill - did everyone get off?" asked Dick.

"I don't know what could've happened, Dick. That stove was getting old. We were all able to get off. We was just about to put the dories over the side when we saw the smoke and flames coming from the galley. It's lucky we had all the dories in the water, so we got off pretty quick," replied Bill.

"The captain is up in the wheelhouse, Bill. Let's go

up and see what we're going to do with you fellers," said Dick.

The crew of the Sally Smith were all standing around the deck wherever they could find a clear space. Their dories had been all brought aboard and stowed on the deck of the trawler. Some of the men were looking toward what was left of their burning schooner as it slipped beneath the waves leaving behind smoke and some burnt wreckage. Many of the other men did not notice the schooner as it disappeared beneath the waves as they were busy looking around the trawler in amazement. Most of these men had only seen one of these trawlers from a distance.

"If they take us to Gloucester with them how is we supposed to get passage back home?" asked one of the young crewmen.

"I imagine they'll take us into somewhere like St. Pierre or Grand Bank. It's not too far for them to steam," replied Art.

Just then Bill and Dick walked over to where the men of the schooner were standing.

"Well men, the skipper has decided that they'll take us into Harbour Breton. It's only a few hours steam for them from here," said Bill.

"That's good to hear - some of the boys was worried we would have to try and get home from Gloucester," said Art.

"Now, boys don't go worrying about that, we'll get you home," said Dick as he went over to Art and shook the hand of his old friend.

The trawler was on her way now to Harbour Breton and would be arriving in the morning. The crew of the schooner all had a good look around the trawler. They had been to the wheelhouse, engine room and down into the holds where the men saw how the fish was stored in bins packed with ice.

Bill and his crew were inside the galley sitting at a table having a cup of coffee. They had just been given a hot meal of beef stew with biscuits. For many of these young men from Harbour Breton, it was their first-time tasting beef that wasn't salted. Coffee was a new experience for many of them, as well. They were also staring at the man who had cooked and served them their meal. It was the first time many of these men had ever seen a black man.

Dick walked over to where Bill was sitting and sat down next to him with a cup of coffee.

"Wel,l Dick b'y, how's Mary and the youngsters doing?" asked Bill.

"They're all doing good, I guess. Times have been hard everywhere these past years. I thought we were going to have to come back home a few years ago but I was able to hold onto my job -, I was one of the lucky ones. Things seem to be getting a bit better. Hopefully, this depression will end soon," replied Dick.

"How are things with you Bill?" asked Dick.

"Oh, pretty good. Martha has her hands full with the boys. Thank God she's got Angie there to help her out, I don't know what we would do without her. Things are bad on the island, Dick b'y. There's no work for anyone. We were all so happy to get back to work and now… we've lost the schooner. We'll all have to go back on the damn dole again. People are sick and starving," replied Bill.

"I know - Mary gets letters from Albert every few weeks and he writes that things have been pretty tough in Harbour Breton," said Dick.

"Things would be a lot worse if it wasn't for Albert, that's for sure. He helps a lot of people outside his working hours especially the ones that can't pay to go see him at the hospital. I don't know what the people of Harbour Breton would have done without him," said Bill.

"Well, I guess I better have a look around before I go to the wheelhouse and relieve the skipper. You fellers will have to sleep out on deck tonight. It's a nice night and not too cold anyway."

"Don't you worry about us, Dick b'y, were a pretty tough bunch," said Bill.

"Yes, that's for sure, Bill, I'll see you in the morning," laughed Dick.

A large crowd had gathered now on the wharf in Harbour Breton. Most of the town had turned out to see why this ship was visiting their community. As the trawler pulled along side the dock, the lines were thrown ashore. The gangway was put out and the crew of the schooner, Sally Smith, started to make their way down onto the dock. Jake started to make his way through the crowd of people and then walked up to where Art was standing.

"What happened, Art b'y?" asked Jake.

"Fire, Jake b'y... the schooner caught fire."

"Did everyone get off?" asked Jake.

"Yes, we was all up and putting the dories in the water for the first set of the day and the next thing we all knew, there was smoke and flames coming from the galley. We was lucky that there was a trawler nearby and they picked us up and brought us in," replied Art.

"Where's Bill?" asked Jake.

"He's still on board talking with Dick," replied Art.

"Dick? Dick who?" asked Jake.

"Dick Snook - that's the boat Dick is mate on," replied Art.

Jake quickly made his way over to the gangway as Bill and Dick were making their way down to the dock.

"Well, Jake b'y, I guess you heard what happened,"

said Bill.

"Yes, thank God everyone got off," replied Jake.

Jake looked at Dick and said, "Thank you so very much for picking up the crew and bringing them home. Is there anything that I can offer you and your captain?"

"No, Jake, I'm happy we were able to help. The captain wants to get under way as soon as we can and head back to Gloucester."

Two short blasts of the ships horn rang out and Dick new that this was the signal for him to get aboard so they could get underway.

"I better get going or he'll leave me here on the dock," laughed Dick. "Tell Albert that I'm sorry I wasn't able to see him."

The men all shook hands. Bill and Jake thanked him again and told him to thank the captain as well. Once Dick walked up the gangway, it was immediately pulled back aboard. Once the lines were let go, the trawler pulled off the dock and prepared to head out into Fortune Bay and into open water to begin their journey home to Gloucester.

Bill and Jake were now standing on the dock with the crew all around them. A large crowd of people had also gathered around to hear what had happened. Everyone listened intently as Bill and the other crew members recounted the tale. Just then John Brown made his way through the crowd.

Everyone moved aside so he could get to where Bill and Jake were standing.

"I heard what happened but there's no way that these men can get a ration now for this month. They'll have to wait for next month. It's not my fault this happened," said John Brown.

Everyone mumbled under their breaths and looked at the man with a mix of astonishment and hate in their eyes.

"What in the name of Christ is wrong with you man? Do you think that anyone can help what happened?" said Jake.

"That's not my problem. Everything has been issued for the month," sputtered John Brown as he turned and pushed his way through the crowd to make his way home.

"That dirty son of a bitch," said Bill

"Someone should beat the piss out of that bastard," said Art.

"Don't worry, men - I can cover you fellers for this month - everyone will get their monthly ration," said Jake.

"Thanks, Jake b'y," said Bill.

Most of the crew along with the people of the town, had left the wharf and were making their way home. Jake looked at Bill and said, "Bill, can I talk with you fer a minute before you head home."

"Yes, Jake b'y." Bill looked towards his son and said, "Lawrence, you go on home and tell your mother I'll be there in a bit."

Lawrence replied, "Yes sir," and then started to make his way home.

"So, what do you think happened? How did the fire start?" asked Jake.

"I'm not sure, b'y...it all happened so fast. George said there was nothing left on the stove and I believe him. That stove was old - maybe something happened to it. I guess we'll never know," replied Bill.

"Yes, I guess we'll never know now. Everyone was able to get off, anyway."

"Well, at least you can get the insurance money," said Bill.

Jake looked out toward the bay and said, "No, Bill b'y. I cancelled the insurance this past winter. We decided not to spend money on insurance again this year. We pay that money every year and never had to use it. Then the minute we cancel it, look what happens," said Jake as he shook his head.

Bill did not say anything.

"Well, at least we don't owe anything on the boat. We haven't been making any money at the fish the past few years. It's the store that's been making a living for us. This is it for me, Bill. Sally and I have been talking about getting out of the fishing business altogether. It's just me and Sally now anyway -

the youngsters are all out on their own. We've saved enough money over the years to be able to get by with just the store. I know that's not going to be any help for you and your family Bill, but I'll do what I can to help."

"Don't worry about us, Jake b'y - as long as me and the boys can get some fish and we can grow some vegetables, we'll survive. Things will be tough, but we'll make it," said Bill.

Bill shook Jakes hand and said, "I better get home... I'll see you later."

Jake said nothing as he turned and walked home to break the news to his wife, Sally.

CHAPTER 4

Daylight was just starting to break as Lawrence Johnston and Joe Hickey walked down a dirt path towards the trail that would lead them to the small fishing stage where Bill Johnston kept his dory. Bill and his sons used the boat to catch the fish they needed to survive these past months because of the abrupt end of the fishing season. It had been a long, hard summer for Bill and his family, but they had fared better than most in the community. The people of Harbour Breton had worked together as much as they could, by sharing fish and vegetables with those of the community that did not have the means to provide for themselves. There had been several more infant deaths in the community that had been attributed to malnutrition. As the young men made there way along, Joe stopped and said, "What's that over there on the side of the road?"

Lawrence looked to where Joe was pointing and said, "I don't know - it looks like someone is laying down. Maybe someone got drunk and couldn't make it home."

The two young men made there way over and stood

next to the person who was laying in the grass. It was starting to get lighter now and as Lawrence looked closer, he said, "By the size of him, it looks like John Brown."

"Yes, there's no one else in the harbour as big as that bastard," said Joe.

The young men leaned down and with some great effort turned over the body of John Brown. The man's eyes were wide open, and the boys could see that there was also dried blood on the side of his face and neck. Lawrence reached down and put his hand on the man's shoulder and gave him a shake but there was no response.

"Is he dead?" asked Joe.

"It looks like it to me...we better get home and get someone. I'll go home and get the old man - you stay here with him," said Lawrence.

"To hell with that, I'm not staying here," replied Joe as both young men turned and ran back to Lawrence's house.

The body of John Brown was now lying in a building next to the cottage hospital that served as a morgue or "dead house" as the people of the community called it. The body was on a slab in the dimly lit, pale white room that had only a few small windows to let in light. Dr. Albert Lewis, who had just finished examining the body, covered the man with a white sheet. Standing off to the side of the room was the town magistrate, Jack Saunders.

"So, Doctor, what do you think happened? Do you think this may be foul play?" asked the magistrate.

"I'm not 100% sure, Jack. I'm not a pathologist or a detective, but there was a blow to the back of his head. Now if those injuries were caused by someone striking him or from him falling, I wouldn't be able to tell you for sure. Have you examined the area where the boys found the body yet?" asked Albert.

"No Doctor, I was planning on doing that later. I guess I'll have to ask around to see if anyone knows anything."

"It could be foul play, or it could have been an accident. The man was certainly hated by many people around here but we both know how drunk he liked to get. Everyone in town has seen him stumbling home at night so it's a wonder he's managed to go as long as he has without having some sort of accident. I would hope that this is some sort of terrible accident and that no one did anything to harm the man. I'll come down with you and have a look at where the boys found the body, just give me a minute to get cleaned up and I'll meet you by the front door. We can leave the body here and come back to look at his wounds again. I may have to do an autopsy to see if there is any damage to the heart. A man his size who lived as hard as he did could certainly be a prime candidate for a heart attack," said Albert.

"Ok then, Doctor, I'll meet you outside. I must get word to St. John's about this. I'm sure they'll be sending a constable to investigate the matter. Seeing that he's a government employee and has died under strange circumstances," replied the magistrate.

Albert removed his white surgical coat and went to a sink to wash his hands. He then went over to a hook near the door and put on his coat. Albert left the building and locked the door behind him.

Albert and the magistrate now looked around the grassy area where the body of John Brown had been found. They did not find anything that could have been used as a weapon. As Albert moved around the tall wet grass, he saw a protruding rock that had what looked like blood on it. A crowd had now gathered, and people were watching Albert and the magistrate intently from a distance.

"Jack, why don't you go and ask anyone if they saw anything last night," said Albert.

"Yes, Doctor, that's a good idea," replied the magistrate as he turned and headed over to where several of the townspeople were standing.

Albert took another look around but did not find anything other than the rock with the blood on it.

The rock would certainly answer for the wounds he found on the back of the man's head but not for the bruises he found on the man's jaw. Albert stood up and stepped out of the grass onto the road. He leaned down and wiped the water and wet grass from the bottom of his trousers. Just then the magistrate walked up to him and said, "A few people saw him last night and they all say he was pretty drunk. Mrs. Quann said she saw him leave his house around ten - she couldn't sleep and was up making a cup of tea for herself. She said she could tell by the way he was stumbling around; he was drunk."

"Well, I guess he could have just fell and hit his head if he was as intoxicated as they say," said Albert.

"I guess I should still ask around to see if there was someone that may have had ill will against Mr. Brown," said the magistrate.

"You may have to talk to the whole community. I don't think there are to many in this town that didn't hate the man. I don't like to speak ill of the dead, but I think we both know what a hateful man Mr. Brown was. Just let me have another look at the body and I'll get back to you. This was most likely just a terrible accident," said Albert.

Both men started to make their way back to the hospital. Just as they walked past the house of Bill and Martha Johnston, Bill walked down to the road to meet the men.

"Good morning, Albert...good morning, Jack...any

idea what happened to the man?" asked Bill.

"We're not sure yet, Bill. We must do a bit more investigating and Jack here will have to speak to a few more people," replied Albert.

"We think it may have been just an accident, but we have to leave no stone unturned," said the magistrate.

"Well, if you need to talk with Lawrence again, just let us know," said Bill.

"I spoke with the boys this morning. I don't think I'll need to talk with them again," said the magistrate.

"Ok then, I'll talk with you fellers later," said Bill as he turned and headed back to his house.

Albert unlocked the door to the building where the body of John Brown was being stored and then both men walked inside. Albert lifted the sheet and began to examine the body again. The magistrate stood back and took notes as Albert began to speak.

"The wound to the back of the head was a result of him falling and hitting his head on that rock that I found protruding from the ground - I'm almost 100% sure of that. It's just this bruise around his jaw. I suppose it could have happened when he fell. There's no real way of knowing for sure," said Albert.

"I'll take your word for it, Doctor. I'll send a wire to St. John's and tell them that we have deemed this to be an accidental death."

Albert paused for a moment and then said, "Yes, I don't think we can say that this was any sort of foul play unless we hear or discover something to the contrary."

"Ok then, Doctor, I'll check and see if Mr. Brown had a last will and testament. We'll need to know what should be done with the body... for burial that is. I know he said that he had no family in Newfoundland and he never mentioned much about England," said the magistrate.

Later that week, the body of John Brown was laid to rest in the Anglican cemetery in Harbour Breton. No will had been found so government officials had instructed the magistrate to have the body buried in Harbour Breton. They had also instructed that Jake Smith should assume the responsibilities of government agent until someone else suitable could be found and sent to the community.

Albert was sitting behind his desk at the cottage hospital preparing to see his last patient of the day. The door opened and young Tom Skinner walked in with his mother following just behind him. Albert thought this strange as the boy was 17 and would have normally come for a visit on his own.

"What can I do for you today?" asked Albert.

"It's Tom's hand, Doctor - I think he broke it," replied Mrs. Skinner.

Albert got up from his chair and went over to examine the boy's hand and as he squeezed it lightly, the boy tried to withdraw his hand and winced in pain.

"Yes, I do believe its broken. I'll have to get a cast on it."

Albert walked across the room and opened the door to his office. He told the nurse to get the materials he needed to put a cast on the boy's hand. As Albert went back to where the boy and his mother were standing, he said, "Now, how did you manage to break that hand, young man?" The boy did not say anything, and he just looked at his mother.

"He fell down when he was bringing in firewood," replied the boy's mother.

Albert said nothing for a moment and just thought to himself that it must have been a hard fall.

"So, Mrs. Skinner, I haven't seen you since your husband passed. How are you and the children getting by?" asked Albert.

"Pretty good, I guess," replied Mrs. Skinner.

Suddenly the young man started to cry.

"What's wrong, Tom - did I hurt you?" asked Albert.

"Stop, Tom, please stop," said Mrs. Skinner as she started to cry as well.

"Ok now, you two, tell me what's going on here," said Albert.

"I didn't want to hit him, but he was trying to hurt Mom," sobbed Tom.

"Who was trying to hurt your mother?" asked Albert.

"Tom, be quiet!" said the boy's mother as she started to sob uncontrollably.

"It was John Brown. I came downstairs and he was trying to hurt mom," said the boy.

Tom could not say anymore as he started to cry.

"What happened, Mrs. Skinner?" asked Albert.

"That awful man showed up at my house drunk the night he died. He told me he would give us back our dole if … I went upstairs with him. I said no and tried to get him to leave and that's when Tom came downstairs. He tried to hit me, and Tom stopped him, hit him in the face and he fell on the floor. But I swear to God we didn't kill him. He got up and just headed out the door and then we went back to bed. The next morning, we heard he was dead. But I swear to God, Doctor, he was fine when he left our house," said Mrs. Skinner.

Albert realized that's where those other marks came from. Albert didn't say anything for a moment and then looked at the boy and asked, "Is this true, Tom?"

The boy replied, "Yes, Doctor, I swear to God. I was

just trying to help Mom."

"I believe you, son. Does anyone else know about this?" asked Albert.

"No, it was just us - the other youngsters don't know either - they didn't wake up that night," replied Mrs. Skinner.

"I don't want either of you to say anything about this to anyone. Neither of you did anything wrong. The man was drunk - he fell, and hit is head on the way home. Tom, you did what any man would have done - you were protecting your mother. That man was a pig and it's no one's fault except his own, that he's dead. I want you both to never speak of this again - am I clear?" asked Albert.

"Yes, Doctor, we won't say anything to anyone else," replied Mrs. Skinner as Tom nodded in agreement.

"Ok, you two, wipe your eyes and take a couple of minutes to calm down," said Albert.

After a few moments, the boy and his mother were ready to leave. Albert said, "Now remember, nothing to anyone about this. Neither of you were at fault for that man's death, but other people that don't know you may not have the same opinion as me" said Albert.

"Yes, Doctor, thank you so much," replied Mrs. skinner.

"Alright…just come back in a month so I can take that cast off."

Albert got up and opened the door so the boy and his mother could leave the room. He then went back to his desk and sat down. Just then the nurse looked in the room and said, "That was your last patient for the day, Doctor."

Albert did not say anything. After a few seconds, the nurse looked at him and asked, "Are you ok, Doctor?"

"I'm fine…just a bit tired. I just need to check a few files before I go home - could you please close the door Sarah?"

The nurse left the room and closed the door behind her. Albert stared out the window for a moment and then got up from his desk, got his coat and headed out the door to go home and see his wife.

Albert was on his way home. It was a sunny September afternoon but there was now that familiar crisp feeling of fall in the air. He looked toward the harbour and saw that the coastal boat was just leaving. The boat made a weekly stop at the community to deliver freight, mail and passengers. Albert opened the door to his house and walked inside. As he opened the door, he was shocked for a moment as he saw his son sitting at the kitchen table with his wife, Cora.

"John, what are you doing home?" asked Albert. A frown came over Albert's face as his son stood up from his chair. Albert could now see that his son was dressed in a military uniform. A feeling of dread came over Albert. He knew full well that war was coming soon as Germany had invaded Poland a few days ago and it would not be long before England declared war.

CHAPTER 5

Albert, Cora and John were sitting at their kitchen table having an evening meal consisting of fresh, fried cod and boiled potatoes that their house-keeper, Jane, had prepared for them. There had not been much conversation during the meal. Albert could not hide his disappointment. John had signed up for the Royal Navy and had received a commission as junior officer. He would be heading back to St. John's in a few days and then off to England to begin his training. Albert had decided that he would not say anything that would have discouraged his son. He new full well that John only wanted to do his part and serve his country just as he himself had done during the first war. Albert only just wished that John had finished his medical studies. He knew better than anyone what was in store for his son. He just hoped to God that the war would not last long. Albert had read that the British and French had a large build-up of troops and were dug in along the Maginot Line. Hopefully, Hitler would stop at Poland. Albert just wished that the boy's uncle, Dick Snook, were still living in Harbour Breton. Albert had served in the trenches and did not have much advice to give his son about wartime naval service. Dick had seen action during the first war and would be better suited to offer advice to John.

"Well, Jane, that was a wonderful meal again tonight," said Cora.

"Thank you, Mrs. Lewis," replied Jane.

"Yes, it certainly was. I think that was the best fried cod I've ever had. Let me help you clear the table," said John.

Jane did not say anything - she just lowered her head, smiled and went about her work.

Albert and Cora looked at each other knowingly. Jane and John were close to the same age. Jane was a beautiful young woman and John was a tall, good-looking young man who always received lots of attention from women. He looked even more handsome now in his uniform.

"That's ok, John. I think Jane can manage on her own. We'll go into the parlor, have some brandy and listen to the radio for a while to see if there's any news about Europe," said Cora.

As they left the room, Albert could see his son glancing back at Jane as she cleared the table. We better keep an eye on those two, Albert thought to himself.

Albert, Cora and John were now sitting in the parlor sipping on their brandy. Albert got up from his chair and went over to turn off the radio. They had just finished listening to the news broadcast. England had declared war on Germany. They all sat in silence for a few moments.

"I'm going to go up and lay down…I'm feeling a bit tired," said Cora as she got up from her chair and headed upstairs to their bedroom.

Albert knew that Cora was upset. Cora also knew what war would mean. She had a brother who had served during the first war and after he returned, he was never the same again. Her brother had started to drink heavily when he returned from Europe and had committed suicide just a few years after the end of the war.

Albert and John sat in silence for a few moments. Albert got up from his chair and went over to the fireplace. He put a piece of wood on the small, smoldering fire and then picked up the fire iron and stirred up the ashes. The fire slowly came back to life and started to crackle as Albert placed the rod back in its holder and sat back down in his chair. Albert picked up his glass of brandy and took a sip.

"Well, I guess there may be a bit of action after all," said John.

"Be careful what you wish for, Son. I've seen war and believe me, it's not what you think it may be. I just hope that this war does not last long," said Albert.

"I know that you and mother are upset but I have to do my part. I can't just sit idly by and let others do all the work," said John.

"I just wish you had finished your medical studies. You would have been able to use your talents and help by saving lives instead of taking them," said Albert.

John said nothing as he lowered his head and took a big gulp of his drink.

Albert looked over at his son and then put his hand on the young man's shoulder.

"Sorry, Son. I'm proud of you...both me and your mother are very proud of you. This is awfully hard on both your mother and me. You're our son, and no matter how old you are, you'll always be our boy and we'll always worry. I must ask you though, why the navy?" asked Albert.

"I don't know. I guess the sea is in my blood - something I got from grandfather, I guess. They're saying that the Newfoundland Regiment won't be going overseas. The government doesn't have the funds to send them. They'll be staying in Newfoundland as a home protection force," replied John.

That wouldn't be so bad - it would certainly be a lot easier on me and Cora, Albert thought to himself as he got up from his chair. Albert took the glass from John's hand and went over to the cabinet to pour himself and his son another glass of brandy. Albert walked back to where his son was sitting, handed him his glass and sat back down in the chair.

Just then Jane, the housekeeper, walked into the room and asked, "Is there anything I can get for you, Doctor Lewis?"

"No, thank you, Jane, we're fine. Cora has already gone to bed and I'll be joining her soon. You can go to your room for the night. We won't be needing anything else this evening," replied Albert.

"Thank you, sir, I'll see you in the morning," said Jane as she smiled and left the room closing the door behind her.

"She seems like a nice girl," said John as he took a sip of his brandy.

"Yes, she is, John. She's a very respectable young woman that's in our employ," replied Albert sternly.

John said nothing as he lowered his head and took another sip of his brandy.

Albert was sitting at his desk going over some files. The nurse opened the door, looked inside and said, "No more patients for today, Doctor."

It had been a terribly slow day. This would be the last day that John would be home. He would be off to St. John's in the morning and then shipping out to England. Albert decided that he would go home early and spend the rest of the day with his son. Cora was at school and would not be home until midafternoon. Albert stacked the papers he was reading on his desk, then got up from his chair, took his overcoat from the coat rack and put it on. He walked out into the hallway and told the nurse that he would be leaving for the day and if they needed him, he would be at home. Albert walked outside - it was a sunny, cool late September day. He took a deep breath, buttoned his overcoat and started to walk the short distance home. These past couple of days had been hard for he and Cora, and they tried not to let John see how concerned they were. Albert and Cora knew it would be a long time before they would see their son again, if they ever did get to see him again, Albert thought to himself. He shuddered as he tried to remove the thought from his mind. Albert walked through the gate and up the path to his house. When he stepped into the porch, he hung his overcoat in the closet, took off his boots and slipped on a more comfortable pair of shoes. He then opened the door and walked into the kitchen. Albert looked around and thought it strange that Jane was not in the kitchen preparing dinner. He walked in the parlor and looked around but did not see John either. I guess he must be out with one of his friend's, Albert thought to himself. As Albert got closer to the stairs, he could hear a noise coming from upstairs. He walked to the top of the stairs and heard a thumping noise coming from John's room. He also heard other noises now and knew why John and Jane were not around - and he new full well what they were up to. Albert banged his fist on the bedroom door. The thumping suddenly stopped and Albert yelled, "You two get dressed and get your arses downstairs, right now!"

Albert was furious - thank goodness it was him that caught them and not Cora, he thought to himself.

Albert was sitting at the kitchen table as John and Jane walked into the room. Jane was fixing her hair and dress. She looked over to where Albert was sitting with his arms folded and started to cry.

"Jane, you go to your room please...I want to talk with John," said Albert.

As Jane started to leave the room, Albert looked at his son and said, "John, I hope you didn't take advantage of that young girl. What, in the name of God, were you thinking? What if it had been your mother and not me, that came home early?"

Jane turned for a moment and said, "He didn't take advantage of me, Doctor Lewis...it was just as much my fault as his."

Jane left and headed into the small room off the kitchen where she slept. Albert looked at his son and said, "Well, what do you have to say for yourself, John? What were you thinking? You know that when your mother finds out, Jane will have to be let go and sent home in disgrace. She'll have to tell her mother why she had to leave our employ and she will never get work as a housekeeper again. Jane will have to toil as a beach girl now and even those jobs are scarce."

John did not say anything for a moment and then he said, "It just happened father, we were talking and well... she's very smart and beautiful. We're only human you know. Please don't tell mother. Let her keep her job. I'll be leaving tomorrow."

Albert was starting to calm down now. He looked at his son, sighed and asked, "How long has this been going on, John?"

"It was just today. It was the first time today... it just happened," replied John.

Albert did not say anything because he knew what it was like to be young. I knew this might happen, he thought to himself. Albert walked over, knocked on the door to Jane's room and said, "Jane, could you please come out here?" The door opened and Jane walked into the room with her head lowered and tears in her eyes.

"Ok now, you two, this can't happen again. I won't tell Cora about what happened here today. Jane, you can keep your job but nothing like this can happen again or you will be fired. Do you understand, Jane?" asked Albert.

"Yes Doctor, I'm so sorry...and thank you, sir," replied Jane.

"Yes, now go get yourself cleaned up and start supper so when Cora gets home, she won't think there's been anything going on. John, you come into the parlor with me," said Albert.

Albert and his son walked into the parlor and Albert closed the door behind them. John started to make his way upstairs to his room.

"Not so fast, young man. Where do you think your going? Get over here and sit down."

John looked at his father and was about to say something but thought better of it and went over and sat down.

"It was no one's fault, Father, it just happened," said John.

"You should know better, John - that girl is in our employ. What if ,God forbid, you get her pregnant?" asked Albert.

"It was only the one time, Father. I know I should have known better, but Jane is a beautiful woman and smart, as well," replied John.

"It only takes once. If something like that were to happen, we'll have to deal with it." Albert sighed and lowered his head. "What is done is done. I'm not going to argue with you on your last day home. God only knows when we'll see you again." Albert went over to a cabinet, got two glasses and poured a drink for himself and his son. He walked over to John, handed him a glass and sat down in the chair next to him.

Both men sat in silence for a moment, then Albert said, "I guess the best advice I can give you before you head off to war, son, is always keep your wits about you. Follow orders but don't do anything stupid. Don't try to be a hero - just do your duty. I wish your Uncle Dick were here. He served in the navy during the first war, you know."

"Yes, I know, Father. They've trained us very well and I'll be getting more training in England," replied John.

"No amount of training fully prepares you for war, John," said Albert.

Just then, the door opened and Cora walked into the room.

Both men were silent for a moment and then Albert spoke, "Hello dear, how was your day?"

"It was good. You're home early today," replied Cora.

"Yes dear, it was a slow day so I thought I would head home early and spend some time with John."

"Well, that was a good idea. I'll head upstairs now and get changed for supper," said Cora as she walked over to her son. She put her hand on John's shoulder and gave him a kiss on the head.

"How was your day, John? What have you been doing all day?" asked Cora.

"John didn't say anything for a moment. He looked down at the floor and said, "Nothing...just laying around all day."

"Are you feeling ok, John Dear? You look a bit flush,"

said Cora.

"He's fine, Dear. It's warm in here and we've had a couple of brandy. You go on upstairs and get ready for supper," said Albert.

"Ok then. I'll see you two in a bit," said Cora.

Albert and Cora were now laying in bed and it was past midnight but neither one of them could sleep.

"It was so hard saying goodbye to him today. I just pray to God this war won't last long and we'll get him back home with us again soon," said Cora.

"I hope so, Dear," replied Albert.

"What happened with John and Jane the other day?" asked Cora.

"What do you mean?" replied Albert.

"I'm not stupid, Dear. I've seen the way those two have been looking at each other. Jane was almost as upset as I was when John left today. It's easy to see that they care for each other."

Albert sighed and said, "When I came home early the other day, I found them upstairs in Albert's room. I didn't want to say anything...they're both young. I didn't want to fire the girl - jobs are so hard to come by. It would ruin the girl's reputation and she would never find work as a housekeeper again."

Cora was silent for a moment and then she said, "I

won't say anything to Jane. I'm sure she was embarrassed enough. It was just as much John's fault as hers, I'm sure. Anyway, we know what it's like to be young."

Albert reached over and put his arm around his wife. She moved from her side of the bed to his and put her head on his chest.

"Yes, we could hardly keep our hands off each other," said Albert as he began to stroke his wife's hair. Cora moved closer to her husband and began to rub her hand over his chest and stomach. Albert turned toward his wife and kissed her.

CHAPTER 6

It was a cold February day and the war had been going on for almost six months. Bill Johnston, Art Hunt and several other men of the community were all standing on the wharf next to the old Newman's store, talking about the previous nights radio address. The men were all either smoking pipes, chewing tobacco or doing a combination of both.

"Well, the call has gone out for volunteers. Did you fellers listen to the radio address last night from Governor Walwyn?" asked Bill.

"Yes, they want men between 20 and 35 that weigh at least 112 lbs, who are in good health and have good eyesight," replied Art.

"They don't want any of us old buggers, then," laughed Bill.

"The only good thing about this war is there will be some work now. The army and navy pay a lot better than the dole. They'll be looking for men to sail on them ships that take men and supplies overseas. They say that the Canadians and Americans will be coming to Newfoundland to build some bases.

They're going to need lots of men to build them bases. Jake was saying they'll be after more wood and iron ore now too, and even the salt fish market might get better. They'll be looking for men in Corner Brook in the woods and Bell Island in the mines," said Art.

"Yes, my boys are all too young to volunteer, but the oldest boys can find some work building those bases. The fishing is going to pick up again in the spring. Jake got a boat lined up. He's going to get her in the spring from Grand Bank. I should be able to get a couple of my boys out fishing with me in the spring," said Bill.

"They said they wants men for them forestry units to go over to cut timber. The Canadians can look for volunteers here too, I guess. You can join the Canadian Navy and Army now. Our government got no money to send the Newfoundland Regiment over this time so they're keeping them home to watch the bases and guard the mines," said one of the men.

"Yes b'y, lots of young men around now with their hands in their pockets. They should have no problems finding volunteers," said Art.

"I better get home - it'll soon be time fer dinner. I don't want the old woman hollering out for me. It'll be nice to get back out at the fish in the spring, that's for sure," said Bill as he puffed on his pipe.

"Alright, Skipper Bill, I'll drop up this afternoon with them turs," said Art.

Bill nodded to the other men and started to make his way home for dinner.

Bill and Martha were sitting at the kitchen table of their home. The wood stove was crackling now as Bill lifted the cover and put a couple sticks of wood into the stove. The wood stove was the only source of heat for their two-story home. Bill closed the lid on the stove and went back over to his chair and sat down. He cut off a piece of Red Stag chewing tobacco and put it in his mouth as he pulled out an old can from under the chair to spit in. The house still smelled of the fresh baked bread that Martha had prepared that morning and now the home was also filling with an aroma of the split pea soup that was starting to simmer away on the stove. They had finished their dinner and the boys were all in the back room talking about the war and what they would volunteer for when they were old enough. The baby was in the crib sleeping and Angie was cleaning up the dishes from dinner.

"Bill, I wish you'd stop chewing that old tobacco," said Martha as she shook her head.

"Now, old woman, don't go keepin' on again," laughed Bill as he spit in the can that was sitting at his feet.

"I'm some glad our boys aren't old enough to go off to that war," said Martha.

"Yes, it'll be five years before Felix is old enough - I hope to God it's all over by then. I know there will be a few men from here heading off soon. When Jake gets the boat in the spring and we gets back at the fish, I should be able to get one of our boys on as cook's helper and maybe one on as doryman," said Bill.

Martha got up from her chair and went over to stir the soup that was simmering on the stove.

"I want to go," said Angie.

Bill and Martha both looked over to where their daughter was standing.

"Go where? It's snowing out and freezing cold. Where do you want to go like this?" asked Martha.

"I think she means something else," said Bill.

"I want to volunteer. They say they're looking for women volunteers, too," said Angie.

"What in the name of God are you talking about?" asked Martha.

"I want to join up. There looking for young women to work as nurses and things like that," said Angie.

"Don't you go talking such foolishness. You can't go away. The men go off to war, not the women," said Martha.

"Bill, tell her to stop talking such foolishness," said Martha.

"Now, Angie my love, listen to yer mother. You need

to stay home and help your mother with the boys until you meet someone and start a family of yer own. I'll be going back at the fish in the spring and your mother will need some help," said Bill.

"I don't want to stay home and do nothing. They need women to help too...the men can't do all the work. It's not like I'll be fighting. I'll most likely just stay in Newfoundland and work at one of the bases. I'll be getting paid for it, you know. I can get my own money and be able to send some money home to help out you and mom," said Angie.

"Now, Angie, that's enough of that talk. We don't want to hear anything else about it," said Martha.

Angie looked at her mother and father with tears in her eyes and said, "I don't care what you say. I'm 18 now and I can go and do whatever I want," Angie suddenly turned and ran from the kitchen and headed upstairs to her room.

As Martha started to get up from her chair to follow Angie, Bill put his hand on his wife's arm and said, "Sit down, Martha...leave her for tonight. We can talk about this again tomorrow when she's calmed down...when we've all calmed down a bit."

Just then the baby started to cry. Martha went over to the crib and picked up the crying child. She sat in the rocking chair and started to rock the baby back to sleep. Bill spit the chewing tobacco from his mouth and went over to the stove, lifted the cover and put in more wood. He then walked over to the cupboard and took down a bottle of Five Star Whiskey and poured himself a drink. Bill went back to his chair, sat down and lit his pipe.

"If she wants to go, you know we can't stop her. She's a woman now and she can do what she wants," said Bill.

Martha did not say anything - she just continued to rock the baby. The child was sleeping again now. Martha got up from her chair, went over to the crib and placed the baby gently back down.

"She's our only girl, Bill. I don't want anything to happen to her. But if she wants to go, then I guess we'll have to give her our blessing." said Martha.

"We can talk to her in the morning," said Bill as he went over to his wife and kissed her on the head.

Albert was sitting in his parlor having a brandy and waiting for the newspaper that he knew would be arriving today along with the weekly mail. It had been almost five months since his son, John, had left for duties with the Royal Navy. In the last letter they had received from John, he had written that he was now serving on a destroyer that was involved with convoy duties. One of their ports of call would be St. John's. There had not been much else information as all the mail was heavily monitored and redacted. It had been a while since they had received the last letter, so Albert was hoping to get one today. The door opened and Cora walked inside with the mail. She was smiling and said, "Here is your paper, Dear, and we have several letters from our John."

Cora sat in the chair next to Albert. She handed him the newspaper and he took it and laid it on the table between their chairs. Cora started to look through the letters. She stopped for a moment, looked at Albert and said, "Well now, I guess one of these letters isn't for us – this one's addressed to Jane."

Albert looked at Cora, smiled and said, "Well then, I guess you better call her in and give it to her."

"I'll take it to her, Albert. I don't want the poor girl to be embarrassed," said Cora as she got up from her chair and went out to the kitchen where Jane was preparing supper. Cora walked over to Jane and said, "Here you are, dear…here's some mail for you."

 "Thank you, Mrs. Lewis, it must be a letter from Mom," replied Jane.

"Not this one, Jane… it's from John." Jane looked shocked and began to blush. She could not look Cora in the eye. Cora put her hand on Jane's arm and said, "It's ok, Dear, don't worry. Just finish up what you're doing and go read your letter. I'm going to read ours now." Cora said as she turned and headed into the parlor. She sat down next to Albert, opened their letter and started to read it aloud.

Dear Father and Mother,

I hope all is well and this letter is not too late in arriving. There are sometimes long delays with the mail so if you do not here from me over several weeks, please do not worry.

I am still serving on the Destroyer Westcott. We are escorting Canadian merchant ships from Montreal and Halifax to England. It has meant long hours for everyone on board. The German U-boats have been highly active. I asked one of the dock workers in St. John's to mail these letters for me so they should not be too heavily edited. We usually stop here in St. John's every month. It would be nice to see you both some time. I managed to go and see the girls the last time we were in port. They seem to be doing very well with school. There are rumours that next time we are back to Newfoundland, we will be here for a week or so for a minor refit. If this happens, I will wire you and maybe you both can come to St. John's.

We have it rather good here on the Destroyer. The U-boats shy away from contact with us. It is the merchant ships that take the brunt of the punishment. Those poor merchant seamen are the ones that have it bad. We lost seven ships during our last crossing. We managed to pick up a few survivors but not many. Those poor men were covered in oil and near death. We have a hard time catching the U-boats before they fire their torpedoes.

I have had a lot of time to think. There is not much else to do to fill the long hours. I guess that you saw the letter that I sent to Jane. I became close to her during my short stay home and have grown quite fond of her. I have sent her a letter asking for her hand in marriage. I am sure now, Mother, that you know what happened with Jane and myself during my time home. I have been thinking about her a lot since I left home. When we come to St. John's, I would like for you to bring Jane with you so we can be married - that is, if she agrees, of course. Please ask her what her decision is and to let me know by wire. I would receive that much quicker than by letter. There is not much else to say other than I miss you both very much and hope that this war ends soon.

Your son,

John

Cora laid the letter in her lap and removed her glasses. She smiled at Albert and said, "Well now, I guess we better go talk with Jane."

"Let's give her some time to think…we can talk to her after supper," replied Albert.

Albert and Cora had now finished their evening meal. Jane came over to the table and started to clear away the dishes. Cora put her hand on Jane's arm and said, "Sit down please, Dear."

Jane looked embarrassed and was silent for a moment.

"Please sit down, Jane," said Albert as he stood and pulled a chair out from the table to allow the young woman to sit.

Jane wiped her hands on her apron and sat in the chair between Albert and Cora.

Cora put her hand on Jane's knee and said, "I see you received a letter from John today as well."

"Yes, Mrs. Lewis, I did," replied Jane.

"John told us in our letter what his intentions were and for us to ask what your answer is," said Cora.

"Yes… Mrs. Lewis…the answer is yes. John has been on my mind since he left for the war. I would be so happy to be his wife," replied Jane.

Both women got up from where they were sitting. Cora wrapped her arms around Jane and gave her a hug. "I'm so happy for you, Dear. We'll send word to John as soon as we can. Once we find out when he'll be in St. John's, we'll all head in to see him together."

Albert now stood up from his chair and said, "Welcome to the family, Jane. We'll be happy to have you as our daughter in law. I know that you and John care for each other very much."

"Thank you very much, Doctor and Mrs. Lewis," said Jane as she began to clear the table again.

"Now, now, we can't have that anymore, now can we? Our future daughter-in-law can't be our maid. I'll give you a hand with the dishes and the housework when I can," said Cora.

"No, Mrs. Lewis, I can keep doing the housework," said Jane.

"No, that's enough - and we don't want to here anymore of this "Doctor and Mrs. Lewis" either. You'll have to call us Albert and Cora from now on," said Albert as they all proceeded to clear the dirty dishes from the table.

"You better write to your mother and give her the good news. This letter from John is several weeks old and we could hear from him any day now. We must be ready to leave at a moment's notice," said Albert.

Jane smiled and said, "Yes, I'll go to my room and

write my mother – I'll get the letter in the mail tomorrow. Goodnight Mr. and Mrs… I mean, Albert and Cora," she said as she smiled and headed to her room and closed the door.

"She's a fine young woman," said Albert.

"Yes, she is…I'm so happy for the both of them," said Cora.

"Let's go to the parlor and have a brandy to celebrate. Maybe we'll get some grandchildren soon," said Albert. Albert kissed his wife and took her hand as they walked into the parlor.

CHAPTER 7

Spring finally arrived after a long, hard winter and the fishermen of Harbour Breton were busy about the work of getting their schooners ready to start the new fishing season. As it had been during World War 1, many of the young men of the town were now away serving with either the military or the merchant navy. Most men that served with the merchant fleet were either too old or too young to serve in the military. These merchant ships were taking the much-needed supplies, equipment and troops to England in support of the war effort. Service in the merchant marine had become an extremely dangerous occupation as there were now many German U-boats active in the North Atlantic. The terrible living conditions that had been brought on during the depression years in Harbour Breton and Newfoundland had started to gradually improve since the beginning of the war. The dole for most people, had become a thing of the past. Many men who were not serving in the military, were away working in places like Bell Island, Grand Falls and Corner Brook. All these men were sending money home now to support their families. The war had caused an increase in demand for the commodities produced in Newfoundland, such as iron ore from Bell Island and wood from the central and western part of the island. There was also an increased demand for what had been the life blood of Newfoundland for many years... the salt-dried cod.

Bills oldest sons, Felix and Leo, were now employed as labourers in the Newfoundland community of Argentia, which was located on the eastern side of Placentia Bay. The United States Government had recently begun construction of a new naval base there. The Americans had received the land under the newly signed US-British Destroyers for Bases Agreement.

Bill and Martha's daughter, Angie, had left home during the winter of 1940 with her parent's blessing. She was serving with the Royal Canadian Air Force Women's Auxiliary in Torbay as a radio operator.

Bills sons, Lawrence and Bill Jr., had finished school the previous year and were going to be fishing with their father this season. One of the young men would have to work as cook's helper and the other would be doryman. There had been much arguing and discussion over this as neither young man wanted to be the cook's helper. Bill made the decision that Bill Jr. would take on the job as doryman and Lawrence would have to be cook's helper as he was the younger of the two.

Jake, who had no plans to get involved in the fishery again, had been convinced to get back into it by his wife, Sally. She knew that this would be a chance for them to build their business back to where it had been before the start of the Great Depression. Jake had purchased a schooner from a retiring merchant in Grand Bank. The schooner had been renamed Mary Smith after their youngest daughter. There had been some discussion about the name change as this was considered bad luck by many fishermen. Jake had told them that he had reached is quota for bad luck these past years so they should be fine. Jake and Sally had decided that if things went well these next couple of years, they would purchase one of the new schooners being built in Lunenburg that was equipped with an engine.

Bill was standing on the deck of the schooner watching his crew go about the last of the necessary preparations to get their vessel ready to sail tomorrow at first light for the fishing grounds. The schooner was old and her best years were behind her, but Bill and his crew were simply happy to be back fishing again. Most of the 18-man crew were from Harbour Breton except for Bill's long time cook and friend, George Parrott, of the community of St. Bernard's, formally know as Fox Cove. Art Hunt would be serving as Bill's mate this year as he had done for the past decades during both the good and bad years. Art had been offered a job as captain with a company out of Grand Bank but he declined, saying that he was happy with the mate's job and did not want to take on the extra responsibility that came with being captain.

Art came up from the holds where he had been supervising the crew as they stowed away the last of the bait. He looked around and saw Bill, then headed over to where he was standing.

"Well, Skipper b'y, it looks like we's all ready to go in the marnin… as long as the weather's good, that is," said Art.

"That's good, Art. Is the grub and bait all stowed away?" asked Bill

"Yes sir, Skipper. We're just getting the last of the fresh water now and then we'll be done for the day. Hopefully, we'll get a fair wind tomorrow and the bloody fog stays away."

"Yes, Art b'y…how are my boys making out?" asked Bill.

"They is doing good, Skipper. Both are hard workers and eager to learn," replied Art.

"Now don't go taking it easy on them just because they're my boys. Treat them like everyone else. If they starts to slack off, let me know and I'll give them a kick in the arse," said Bill.

Art laughed and said, "I don't think we needs to worry about that, Skipper, but if they do slack off any, I'll tear a strip off them."

"Ok, Art b'y. I guess we can all head home for the night. It'll be our last night home fer a few weeks."

"Yes sir, Skipper…it feels good to get back at the fish again," said Art as he walked over to where his crew were standing. He told them to finish up for the day and head home to see their families.

Bill was sitting in his kitchen smoking his pipe and having a drink of whiskey. It would be his last drink for a while as he would be back on the water again for at least five or six weeks. Martha had just finished the dishes and put the baby to bed. All the boys were in bed now, even Lawrence and Bill Jr. were sleeping. It had been a long, hard day of work for the boys and they were excited to start their first trip fishing on the Grand Banks with their father. Bill knew that the work would only get harder for his sons, but he also knew that they were up for the task. Martha poured herself a cup of tea and sat down in the chair across the table from Bill.

"Well now, all the boys are sleeping. I guess we can finally read our letter from Angie," said Martha as she put her cup on the table, wiped her hands on her apron and proceeded to open the letter from their daughter.

Dear Mom,

I hope all is well with you, Daddy and the boys. Things are still going well here but we have been very busy. There are more and more planes and men showing up every day. There is not much else to do other than work. We get a weekend leave every couple of weeks so we all usually head into St. John's for a break when we can. The winter was long, and we could not get out for our leave. The snow is all gone now, and we can get into St. John's again, so everyone is happy about that.

The Americans are here now; they came early in January with a new type of airplane that they hope will have better luck finding the U- Boats. There was some trouble at first with the Canadians and Yanks. They did not get along too well. There were a few fights, but things are going much better now. The Canadians treat us locals very well and they are happy to have us here with them.

I hope you got the money that I sent with my last letter. I will be sending more when I get paid at the end of the month. I have some news for you both. I have been seeing an American pilot. His name is Harold Storey or Hal, as everyone calls him. He is a nice man, Mom, and treats me with respect. I hope that you and Daddy will get to meet him soon. We have been spending a lot of time together. I have come to love him very much and he has told me that he wants us to be married. I said yes, but we will have to wait until the war is over to be married. We are both trying to get a week of leave this summer so that I can bring him home to meet you all.

Hopefully, this war will end soon. Thank God that none of the boys are old enough yet to volunteer. I hope the war is over before that happens. I know you and Daddy may be shocked to hear about me getting married but I know you will both like him very much. I just hope that the boys do not scare him off. Please tell them to be on their best behaviour when we get there.

Well, I guess that's all I have to tell you for now. I love you and miss you all. Please do not worry - things are going very well for me here. Please write me soon and let me know how things are going at home. I guess that Daddy is happy to be back fishing. I know you said in your last letter they would be starting again soon.

Your loving daughter,

Martha removed her glasses and looked over at her husband. They both looked at each other in silence for a moment and then Martha said, "Well, I wasn't expecting to read that. I hope she knows what she's doing. What are the Americans doing there anyway - they're not in the war."

"Our Angie knows what she's doing, Mart. I trust her judgement. I'm sure he's a good young man. She's almost twenty years old now so she can make her own decisions. I just hope that I can get to meet the young feller. We'll be fishing all summer so I might not be home when they come to visit. The Americans aren't fighting yet but they're supplying England with a lot of help and equipment. I'm sure it's only a matter of time before the Americans get in the war."

Tears started to fill Martha's eyes as she put down the letter and began to cry.

"Now, Dear, there's nothing to worry about," said Bill.

"I'm not crying because I'm worried...I'm happy for her...that's all. She'll be gone to the States with him when the war is over and God only knows when we'll get to see her again," said Martha.

"Now we can't go worrying about that - I'm sure they'll get back for a visit. We better get to bed. We'll be heading out tomorrow at first light. I hope the weather is good and there's not too much fog. Now, let's get to bed, old woman - it'll be a month or so until I gets to see you again. Sure, we can have another baby if you wants. Maybe we'll have another girl," laughed Bill.

Martha wiped the tears from her eyes with her apron, smiled and said, "Ahhh, stop your foolishness, old man. Get to bed and I'll be up in a few minutes."

John Lewis and Jane Blagdon were married just a few weeks after John's letter proposing marriage had arrived. Once Albert and Cora had received word that John was in St. John's and would be there for a couple of weeks, Albert, Cora and Jane immediately traveled there to meet him. John and Jane were married a few days later. There had been a small ceremony with just Albert, Cora and their daughters attending along with a couple of John's shipmates. The honeymoon for the young couple had been short. After a week into the ship's repairs, John received notice that he would be promoted and would have to immediately sail for England to join the newly built destroyer, HMS Partridge. A few weeks after John had left for England, Jane received a letter from him containing the disappointing news that the Partridge would not be in the North Atlantic but would be conducting operations in the Mediterranean. After their marriage, the plan had been for Jane to move to the city so she would be close when John's ship docked in St. John's. These plans all changed after the news about John's promotion and transfer. Jane was still living with her in-laws at Harbour Breton. Cora and Albert had wanted to hire a new housekeeper, but Jane was having none of that. Jane had told them that if she would be living with them, she would want to help as much as she could. Jane continued to share the household duties with Cora. Cora helped with the cooking and cleaning duties during her time off from teaching.

Albert, Cora and Jane had just sat down to the kitchen table for their breakfast. Albert and Cora started eating their toast and porridge. After a few moments, Cora looked at Jane and noticed that she was not eating any of her meal.

"You're not eating your breakfast, Dear. Are you feeling ok?" asked Cora.

Jane said nothing, then suddenly she jumped up from her chair and ran outside. Cora and Albert looked at each other then got up from the table and followed Jane outdoors. Jane had made it halfway to the outhouse. She was now bending over and vomiting in the grass. Albert went over to Jane and put his hand on her shoulder.

"Are you ok, Jane, my love?" asked Albert.

"I don't know what came over me. It just came on me so fast," replied Jane.

Albert looked at his wife. Cora smiled and gave him a knowing look.

"Come inside, Jane. I'll get you some tea to help sooth your stomach," said Cora.

They all went back inside the house. Jane excused herself and said she was going to lay down in her room for a bit.

"Well, maybe we'll be having that grandchild sooner than expected," said Albert.

"Now, we don't know that for sure, I'll have a talk with her before I go to school. Why don't you go on to the hospital and I'll let you know what she says," said Cora.

"You can ask her if she's had her time of the month yet," said Albert.

"Now, Albert, a woman doesn't always need a doctor to tell her she's having a baby," said Cora.

"Ok then, Doctor. When I come home for dinner today you can let me know what she said," laughed Albert.

Albert went to the coat rack and put his overcoat on. He placed his hat on his head as he went over to his wife to gave her a kiss, then turned and headed out the door.

Cora had just finished cleaning the dishes when Jane

walked back into the room.

"How are you feeling?" asked Cora.

"Much better now. I don't know what could have come over me," replied Jane.

"Sit down, Dear. I have a few minutes before I leave for school," said Cora.

The women each pulled out a chair and sat down at the kitchen table.

"You should try and get some toast and tea after I leave, Jane, even if you don't feel like eating," said Cora.

"The women sat in silence for a few seconds, then Cora looked at Jane, put a hand on her arm and asked, "Have you started your time of the month yet, Dear?"

Jane looked puzzled and after a few seconds, put her hand to her mouth and asked, "Oh my, do you think I might be?"

"Well, if you haven't had your period and you're having morning sickness, those are two good indications that you may very well be," replied Cora.

Jane started to cry. Cora got up from her chair and went to Jane. She put her arms around Jane and said, "It's ok, Dear...everything will be ok."

"I know - I'm just so happy," said Jane as she wiped her eyes. "I'll write John and my mother and give them the news."

"Yes, you should do that. I must get to the school now. Just remember to get yourself something to eat," said Cora.

"I will," said Jane as both women hugged again. Cora smiled, put on her coat and headed out the door.

CHAPTER 8

The crew of the schooner, Mary Smith, were finishing up the last trip of the 1942 fishing season. The war was still raging in Europe, and in the Pacific as well, as a result of the attack on Pearl Harbour by Japan in December of 1941. The fish had been plentiful since Bill and his crew had started fishing again during the spring of 1941.

Skipper Bill Johnston looked on as his crew pulled the last dory back aboard and set about the work of cleaning, splitting, salting and storing the last of their catch. Both his sons, Lawrence and Bill, had done very well since the start of their first fishing trip last year and had continued to do so this year. Bill was immensely proud of his boys. They continued to pull their weight and work just as hard as any man aboard the schooner. Lawrence was now doryman; he had only spent his first year as cook's helper. Two crewmen from the previous fishing season had signed on for service in the merchant marine and as a result, Bill had given his son one of the doryman positions. Bill looked around and thought to himself that the old schooner had served them well these past couple of seasons. Bill and the crew would be heading up to Lunenburg in the spring to bring back the new schooner that Jake was having built in the boat yard there. Having a schooner with an engine would take some getting use to for Bill and his crew. They would also have to carry an extra crewman now. Jake had hired a man from St. John's that would operate and maintain the engine. Jake had also told Bill that it would not be long before they would be icing their catches in the holds instead of salting it. Electricity was coming to more and more parts of the island of Newfoundland.

Many parts of the world had been devastated by the Second World War, but it had been somewhat of a godsend for the people of Newfoundland. The Canadians along with the Americans had brought great improvements to the infrastructure of the island. More roads and rail lines were being built, and there was an improvement to the health care system as well. Electricity had started to come to many parts of the island now. There was also a lot of work for the men and women of the island that were not away serving in the military or in the merchant marine. Newfoundland had not escaped the ugly side of this war, though. Many of the island's young men lost their lives in the navy, merchant marine and regular British army units. Even though the Newfoundland Regiment had not been sent overseas, they were still involved in the war effort. The regiment was providing security for the bases, mills and mines around the island. They were also now training men for service in two British artillery regiments. Newfoundland was also financing an air squadron that provided night air defence for England. Newfoundlanders along with Polish and French personnel served in this squadron.

The war had also hit close to home - Newfoundland had been the recent target of attacks from German U- Boats. Several torpedoes had been fired into St. John's harbour during March of that year but there had been no damage inflicted during the attack. There had also been several cargo ships that had been fired on and sunk around Bell Island which resulted in the deaths of 60 sailors. During October, the war hit even closer to home as a U- Boat that had been operating in the Gulf of St. Lawrence had fired on and sunk the passenger ferry, Caribou, resulting in the deaths of 136 men, women and children. It had been devastating for a local family - Richard Skinner (son of John and Elizabeth Skinner) and his family had been among the casualties.

Bill had decided to finish up their last trip of the season where they had started their fishing season for so many years; on the Saint Pierre Banks. It had been another good year fishing and all the crew would do well financially as a result of the bountiful catches. The prices had increased for the salt cod so the crews, owners and merchants were all reaping the benefits.

The crew were finishing up the work of cleaning up

the deck and securing the dories. They would be lifting the anchor soon and getting underway for home. The sun was starting to set now, and the wind was starting to pick up just a bit. There had been light winds most of the day from the west, but the wind was starting to change and come around from the northeast.

"Ok, men, let's get this old girl underway and then we can head down for some supper," yelled Bill.

Some of the crewmen started to head up forward to pick up the anchor while the rest prepared to set the sails. Just then there was a noise that sounded like a whale breaking the surface of the water for air. Bill and several of the other men looked in the direction the noise had come from but it was almost dark now so the men could not see much.

"There's something over there on the water but it don't look like any whale I ever seen before," said Art as he pointed to the port side of the schooner.

Just as Art had finished speaking, a loud voice boomed out into the cold night air.

"Everyone stand by and prepare to be boarded," a voice boomed in a heavy foreign accent. As the object got closer to the schooner, Bill could see that he and his crew were in grave trouble. Bill recognized what was floating just a few hundred feet off their port beam - it was a German U-Boat.

The large deck gun that was being manned by several bearded, scruffy-looking men, was pointing directly at them. A small boat pulled away from the U-Boat and quickly made its way alongside and four armed, uniformed men quickly climbed aboard the schooner.

"Don't try to do anything stupid and no one will be hurt," said a German officer in a heavy accent.

The crew of the schooner were all in shock and no one said anything as they were all ordered at gun-point to sit down on the deck.

"Which one of you men is the captain?" asked the officer.

Bill stepped forward and said, "Me, I'm the skipper."

"Tell your men to get the small boats ready and put them in the water. Get two of your men to go below and get water and some food to take with you in your boats," ordered the German.

Bill looked toward Art and George, and told them to do what the man had said. He then told the remain-der of his crew to put the dories in the water.

"Three boats will be enough," said the German.

As the armed men looked on in silence, the crew of the schooner boarded the dories. The crew divided themselves equally among the three boats. One of the German crewmen passed down the buckets of water and food that George and Art had collected from the galley. The German officer said something to the other men in German. They then put their guns over their shoulders. One man headed into the galley and the other headed down to where the fish was stowed. The Germans started to load their boat with as much food and salt cod as they could carry. Then they all boarded their boat except for the German officer. He looked down at Bill and said, "Tell your men to start rowing away from your vessel. You and your crew should be fine…we will send a radio message with your position when we are safely away. One of your Tommy or Canadian destroyers will pick you up in the morning." The German officer tipped his hat as he turned and walked away.

Lawrence started to say something under his breath, but Bill gave his son a look. Lawrence knew the look well, so he lowered his head and said nothing.

"All right, tie these dories together and start rowing!" yelled Bill.

Once the dories were all secured together, the crew started to row away from their schooner. When Bill and his crew were a few hundred feet away, the German officer boarded their boat with his men and headed back to the U-Boat. Once the Germans were back aboard, the officer said something to the crewmen manning the gun. Suddenly a bright flash and a loud bang filled the night sky. The shell hit the schooner, Mary Smith, just at the water line amidships. Large splinters of wood flew up into the air and after just a few minutes, the schooner slipped beneath the water. The crew of the U-boat secured the gun and disappeared one by one down into a hatch near to where the gun was located. The hatch closed and then the U-boat turned away and disappeared beneath the waves.

The crew of the schooner were all still in shock and for a few moments, no one said anything.

"Those dirty bastards. I wonder if that's the one that sunk the Caribou," said Art.

"It could very well be - they never got the bastards that done it," said Bill.

"We's lucky they let us go. They could have sent us to the bottom with the schooner," said one of the other crewmen.

"Do you think that he's really going to send a message for someone to come and pick us up?" asked Art.

"I don't know, Art b'y...hard to say what he might do. They didn't kill us all, so maybe he'll do what he said he would," replied Bill.

It was dark now and starting to get considerably cold. It was a clear night with a full moon and lots of stars to light the night sky.

"Ok, men we got our compass - let's start rowing. We can't stay here and hope that someone will find us. We can't count on that German keeping his word either. We got some water and a bit of grub. We'll have to ration what we have in case they don't find us fer a few days. I know we're not too far from Saint

Pierre because I took our position this afternoon. We'll hopefully see another schooner on the way in. We can take turns rowing and when yer not rowing, try and get some sleep," said Bill as he buttoned his jacket and pulled his cap down over his ears.

"Did anyone get a lamp and some matches?" asked Art.

No one said anything so everyone knew the answer.

"All right, check the compass and start rowing north," said Bill.

The sun was finally starting to rise. It had been a long, cold night for Bill and his crew. They had rowed all night but not many of the men had been able to sleep. It was starting to get a bit warmer now as the sun rose higher into the morning sky. Bill looked on as the cook passed out a ration of food and water for his men. They had all been given some dried fish and hard tack along with a cup of water.

Bill looked over to where his sons were to see how they were doing. Both young men were in the dory next to him and they looked to be doing fine. They were both young, healthy and strong. The men had rowed through the night. Bill did not know how much headway they had made through the night as there was no land in sight and his sextant and charts had gone to the bottom with the schooner. The men continued to row and around lunch time one of the crew hollered out, "There's a ship!"

Bill looked to where the crewman was pointing and could see the smoke from a ship on the horizon. Bill picked up a gaff and tied his coat to it and started to wave it in the air. With any luck the ship would be heading in their direction and they would be spotted and picked up, Bill thought to himself.

A Canadian destroyer was now just a few hundred feet away from Bill and his crew. There were several crewmen from the ship looking toward the men in the dories. One of them lifted a megaphone to his mouth and began to speak.

"We are a Canadian destroyer. We received a message giving us your position. We won't be stopping to pick you up as this may be a trap set by the enemy U-boat that sank your schooner. We have radioed to St. Lawrence and given them your position. Please stay on your course as well as you can. There's a trawler on the way and should be here within the next couple of hours." The man waved as the frigate got under way with a loud rumble from the engines and a cloud of black smoke billowing from her stacks.

"How come they didn't pick us up?" asked Bill Jr.

"You heard what he said - it could be a trap for them fellers. When they're stopped dead in the water like that, it makes them an easy target for the U-Boat. Them German bastards could have sunk us and sent the message just to get them here to sink them," replied Skipper Bill.

The crew continued to row but were not making any headway. They were now battling a head wind and a strong current. It would be dark again in just a few hours. Bill did not let on to his crew, but he was starting to worry. Bill knew that the wind and tide was taking them further away from land. He wished that they had more time to grab more items from the schooner before they had been set adrift. If they were not picked up before dark, the trawler would have a hard time finding them and God only knows how far the wind and tide would continue to take them away from land.

Bill looked at the cook, George, and asked, "How much water and grub do we have left?"

"We still got a few buckets of water left. The hard tack will be gone by tomorrow, but we still got lots of dried fish," replied George.

Having only dried fish would not help with the water situation as they had no way to soak and cook the fish to remove some of the excess salt. If they were in the boats long enough to run out of dried fish, they had a couple of hand lines that would allow them to try and catch some fresh fish.

"We'll have to cut back the water to a half cup a day per man until we get some rain, or they pick us up," said Bill.

"Only having dried fish to eat isn't going to help... we'll all die from thirst," said one of the crewmen.

"That's enough complaining. We's all going to be lucky to get out of here alive. We could drift out to the middle of the Atlantic if this wind and tide don't change," said Bill angrily.

The men were all silent as they began to realize the gravity of their situation.

"Look over there to the south!" yelled Art. Everyone looked – they could see the sails and running lights of a schooner that was heading in their direction. Bill picked up the oar and started to wave it in the air.

The schooner lowered their sails and slowly came to a stop alongside the crew of the "Mary Smith". Bill and his men began to row and pulled up alongside the schooner. The crew of the schooner reached down and one by one, pulled Bill and his men aboard their vessel.

Bill, his crew and their dories, were now all aboard the schooner. The schooner was from the Fortune Bay community of St. Jacques. Bill knew the skipper and a few of his crew.

"What happened, Bill b'y?" asked the Captain.

"I don't know if you'd believe me if I told you," replied Bill.

That next morning the schooner pulled alongside the wharf in Harbour Breton and Bill, his crew and their dories were put ashore. Bill and his crew thanked the men that had rescued them. The schooner then drifted off the dock and proceeded to get under way for the short trip to St. Jacques. There was no one from the community on the dock as it was early on a Sunday morning and most people were still sound asleep in their beds. "You men better go on home. I'll head over to Jake's house and break the news to him. My God, he's had a run of bad luck these past few years. The fire and now this. Things were going so good this year," said Bill as he shook his head. "Lawrence, Bill...you two go on home and tell your mother I'll be home in a bit," said Bill.

Bill then turned and made his way toward Jake's house so he could break the bad news to him.

Bill walked up to Jake's house and knocked on the door. After a few moments, the door opened and Jake looked at Bill and said, "Bill...I wasn't expecting to see you fellers yet."

"I'm sorry, Jake b'y...but we've had some more bad luck," said Bill.

"Come inside, Bill, so we can talk," replied Jake

Bill recounted to Jake and Sally everything that had happened. Jake, Sally and Bill all sat in silence for a few moments. "I'm going to make us some tea," said Sally as she got up from her chair and headed to the kitchen.

"I'm sorry, Jake b'y, I lost another schooner," said

Bill as he shook his head.

"Now, Bill b'y, it's not your fault with this one or the last one. It's war time and your lucky that German let you fellers get off first and didn't send you all to the bottom with the schooner. The fire was my fault for not having replaced that old coal stove. At least I got insurance on this one and we is covered for an act of war, too. The main thing is you fellers all got off and no one was hurt. This was going to be the last trip for the year anyway. We'll be getting the new boat in the spring. I was going to try and sell the old schooner anyways. I'll get the insurance money for the schooner and cargo. When I get the money, I'll give you fellers what you're owed for your fish," said Jake.

"Thank you, Jake b'y...you're a good man. I wouldn't blame you if you wanted to get another skipper for the new one," said Bill.

"Stuff like that happens, Bill b'y. Both times no one died, and you got the men all home safe, so that's all that matters."

"Thank you, Jake. I better get home - the old woman will be all worked up fer sure when the boys tells her what happened," laughed Bill.

"Just think about the stories we'll have to tell our grandchildren," laughed Jake.

The men shook hands and Bill headed home to see his wife and family.

CHAPTER 9

Dr. Albert Lewis was sitting in his parlor holding his nine-month-old grandson, John Jr. He looked on as Cora and Jane put the last of the decorations on their Christmas tree. Having a baby in the house had helped Albert and Cora get into the Christmas spirit this year. Their two daughters would be home from St. John's in just a few days and Jane's widowed mother would be arriving from Boxy soon, to spend Christmas with them as well.

The year 1942 was coming to an end and there were no signs that the war would be ending anytime soon. The war was also starting to hit closer to home for the people of the island of Newfoundland. There had been more attacks near Bell Island and there had also been a terrible disaster in St. John's. A fire had occurred at a Knights of Columbus hostel where recruits for the Newfoundland Regiment and other military personnel were being housed. This fire had resulted in the deaths of 99 people and 109 people had been critically wounded. Rumours were rampant that this was the work of enemy saboteurs. There had been other similar incidents that had recently occurred involving other military sites around the St. John's area. The U-Boats were also still highly active in the Atlantic resulting in many more allied ships being lost. The German "Wolf Packs" as they had become known, seemed to be able to operate unchecked.

Albert continued to rock the baby who had been sleeping for the last hour. Jane and Cora started to laugh at something Cora had said and then the baby started to cry. Jane put the ornament on the tree that was in her hand and walked over to where Albert was sitting and took the baby from his hands.

"I know that cry - I think he's hungry," said Jane

"He's got his fathers appetite," said Cora. Albert got up from the chair and looked toward his wife. He could see that there were tears in his wife's eyes. Jane left the room with the crying baby and headed out to the kitchen to feed him. Once Jane left the room with the baby, Albert walked over to where his wife was standing. He put an arm around her shoulder and asked, "Are you ok, my love?"

"Yes, I'm just thinking about John. I always miss and worry about him, but it's always worse this time of year," replied Cora.

"The girls will be home in a few days. That will cheer you up, I'm sure."

"Yes, I know. We haven't received a letter from John in quite some time either. It would be nice to get a letter before Christmas…that would make me feel better. I know that Jane is starting to worry, too," said Cora.

"I'm sure we'll hear something from him soon. The mail has always been slow but with the war going on, it's slowed delivery down to a snail's pace," said Albert as he put his arms around his wife, gave her a hug and kissed her on the head.

"I've just been having this awful feeling lately and I've been dreaming about him almost every night," sobbed Cora.

"Come, let's go and get some supper…maybe we'll get a letter with the mail tomorrow," said Albert as he took his wife by the hand and led her into the kitchen.

The door to the kitchen opened, Albert walked inside and brushed the snow from his jacket and hung it up on the coat rack. He took his boots off and put them next to the stove so they would dry out. Cora and Jane were sitting at the kitchen table having some tea. Albert looked toward the women and smiled as he removed two letters from his pants pocket. "Does anyone want some mail?" Albert laughed. Cora and Jane both got up from their chairs and quickly went over to Albert.

"Here you are…one for you…and one for you," said Albert as he handed each woman their letter.

"I'm going upstairs to check on the baby and then I'm going to lay down and read my letter," said Jane as she smiled turned and headed upstairs to her room.

"Let's go to the parlor, Dear, and read our letter. I'll get us each a glass of brandy," said Albert.

Albert and Cora walked into the parlor. Cora sat in her chair and Albert went over to the fireplace to put a few pieces of wood on the fire. The fire came to life and crackled as he went over to the cabinet, took out a couple of glasses and poured a drink of brandy for himself and Cora. Albert put his wife's drink on the table that was between their chairs and then sat down. Cora opened the letter. "This letter is two months old. Better late than never, I guess," she said as she began to read.

Dear Mother and Father,

I hope you are both doing well during these awful times. I recently heard the news about the U-Boat attacks around Newfoundland. This war is a terrible thing. I hope, as I know you do, that this war ends soon. We are still conducting our convoy duties in the Mediterranean. It certainly has its perks as the weather is much nicer here than in the North Atlantic, especially during the long, hard winter months. We get the occasional shore leave in Gibraltar and now Malta, although there is not much to see in Malta as it has been heavily bombarded over the last few years. I would gladly give up the sunny skies and calm seas to be near home again.

I did not say anything to Jane in my letter as not to get her hopes up, but I have put in for a transfer to the Atlantic theatre of operations again. With any luck, it will be approved in the new year and I may start getting the odd visit to St. John's again. Hopefully,

I will get some news on this before Christmas. It would be nice to see you, mother and the girls again. It would be especially nice to see Jane again and of course, to see John for the first time. I was so happy to receive the picture of Jane and the baby that you sent to me. I always keep it close by. The hope of getting to see my son for the first time gets me through the long days and nights.

There are a couple more lads here from Newfoundland, but they are among the enlisted men and fraternization among officers and regular crew is frowned upon. I should have joined the Canadian Navy, I guess - they say that things are a bit more relaxed on those ships. That was quite the story that Father told me in your last letter about Skipper Bill and his crew's run-in with that U-boat. They are lucky to be alive. This war has taken a hard toll on merchant shipping.

I guess that is all for now as I must go on watch soon. I look forward to receiving more letters from both of you, and Jane.

Your son,

John.

Cora folded the letter put it back in the envelope and laid it on her lap. She then looked toward Albert and began to cry.

"I wish this dam war would end," said Cora.

"I know, my love, come here," said Albert as he reached over and put his arm around his wife to try and comfort her. There was a knock on the door.

"I wonder who that could be - someone must be sick. I'll go and check, Dear, you stay here," said Albert.

After a few moments Albert came back into the room. He was holding a telegram in his hand and looked pale as a ghost. Just then Jane came back down the stairs - she was smiling, until she saw the look on both Albert and Cora's face. Cora got up from her chair and went to Jane. She took Jane's hand, led her to where Albert was sitting and both women sat down next to him. Albert slowly opened the telegram and began to read it to himself. Both women knew from the look on Albert's face that it was not good news. After a few seconds, Albert began to read the telegram aloud to the women. "We regret to inform you...stop...that the British destroyer HMS Partridge has been torpedoed and sunk in the Mediterranean Sea...stop...your husband Lieutenant John Lewis has been listed as missing in action...stop..."

The telegram slipped from Albert's hand and fell to the floor as both women started to sob uncontrollably.

Bill and Martha had just sat down to the kitchen table. The youngest boys were sleeping, and the rest of the boys were in the back room playing cards. Martha had just finished cleaning up from supper. She went over to the stove, picked up the kettle and poured herself a cup of tea. She then went over and sat down on the day bed next to Bill, who was sitting in his chair smoking his pipe.

"I can't wait for Felix and Leo to get home for Christmas. It's been so long since we seen them. I just wish Angie and Hal could make it home," said Martha.

"Yes, it would be nice to see them too," said Bill.

"I wish this war would end soon. In another couple of years, Felix and Leo will be old enough to sign up. I hope it's all over by then. Thank God they kept them both on to work at that base in Argentia," said Martha.

"Lawrence and Bill keep asking me if they can join up for the Merchant Navy. I told them no again this time because I need them both fishing with me in the spring. I don't know how much longer that's going to work. A lot of their buddies are going away in the spring. There are more merchant ships getting sunk than navy ships. Poor Mary and John's boy, Tom, was killed on that tanker they sunk last week just off Cape Saint Mary's. Not even one of the crew got off that one alive…30 men were lost," said Bill.

"I just hope it's all over soon. It's bad enough having Angie away. Now my brother, Mike, is away, working on those merchant ships," said Martha.

"We won't be able to keep Felix and Leo home for much longer. They want to do their part like everyone else. Lawrence and Bill won't be old enough to do anything for a few more years yet," said Bill.

"I don't want to think about that. That's awful about John Lewis. Poor Dr. Lewis and Cora. And that poor, young wife and her baby," said Martha as she shook her head.

"I was talking with Albert the other day. All the telegram said was that he was missing in action and they haven't heard anything else since. Maybe someone picked him up from the water and they didn't hear anything yet," said Bill.

"Well, I guess we better read our letter from Angie," said Martha as she put down her tea, opened the envelope and removed the letter. She unfolded the letter and took out money that Angie had put inside. Martha then put the money on the table and started to read.

Dear Mom,

I hope all is well with you, Daddy and the boys. Things are still going well here. I wish I could get home for Christmas, but I could only get a few days leave. Things are going very well with me and Hal. He still talks about our week in Harbour Breton and how much he enjoyed meeting you all. Hopefully, we will be able to get out for a visit again this summer.

There is a lot of activity here these days with all the planes and pilots. The planes that fly from here are the ones that hunt for the U-Boats. These new planes that the Americans have brought seem to be having more luck tracking and sinking some of the U-Boats. I guess you may have already read in the paper about Hal's friend Donald. He is the American pilot that sank that U-Boat. I was operating the radio when he sent his message "Sighted Sub. Sank Same." It was a great boost to morale here for everyone as there had not been much luck finding U-Boats. They hope to have a road by next year connecting our base to St. John's.

I have enclosed a bit of extra money this time to help with Christmas so you can get a few extra treats for the boys. Hal gave me a bit of money as well. I did not want to take it at first, but he insisted. Hal and I have told the story to everyone about Daddy and his crew's run-in with that U-Boat in the fall. It is quite the story,

117

and everyone enjoyed hearing it. It is lucky no one was hurt. Many of those poor merchant sailors do not fare as well.

Well, I guess that's it for now. I hope you all enjoy your Christmas. Give the boys all a hug for me. I look forward to hearing from you soon.

Your daughter,

Angie

Martha folded the letter and put it on the table. Bill and Martha sat in silence for a few moments and then Bill said, "Well, it sounds like they are doing good. I hope we can get to see them again this summer."

"Yes, it was nice of Hal to send that money. He didn't have to do that," said Martha.

"Angie found a good man for herself. I hope this war will be over soon so they can get married and start a life for themselves," said Bill as he got up from his chair. He went over to the stove, lifted the cover and put in some more wood.

"Its going to be a cold night - I better fill up the stove before I go to bed." said Bill. Just then there was a loud bang followed by noise coming from the back room.

"Bill, you better go check on the boys...it sounds like they're fighting again."

Bill put down the cover for the stove and opened the door to go to the back room where the boys were playing cards.

♦ ♦ ♦

Albert and Cora were sitting in the parlor. The house was quiet now, as their daughters had left yesterday and returned to school in St. John's. Janes mother had also returned to Boxy a few days ago. Jane and the baby were upstairs sleeping. There had not been much celebrating this Christmas. They still did not know if John was dead or alive. They had all tried to make the best of things for the sake of the girls and the baby. Cora and Jane had taken the tree down this morning and they had all just finished eating their lunch. Even though it was only the day after New Years, they had all decided to take down the tree. Albert got up from his chair, went over to the fireplace, picked up the poker and stoked the fire. The fire crackled as Albert went back to his chair and sat down. He then picked up a book and started to read. Cora went over to a small table in the corner of the room and picked up a ball of yarn and knitting needles. She then sat down in her chair and started to knit. Just then there was a knock on the door. Albert put down his book, got up from his chair and went to answer the door. After a few moments, Albert returned to the room. He was carrying an envelope in his hand. It was a letter from the Royal Navy. Albert was consumed with dread as he looked at Cora. He walked across the room and slumped down in his chair. Cora looked and saw who the letter was from. Tears started to well up in her eyes. They both realized that this may be the news that they had been dreading, telling them that their son was now presumed dead.

"I better go get Jane. This letter is addressed to her," said Albert as he slowly got up from his chair. Cora nodded her head in agreement. Albert went upstairs to wake his daughter-in-law. After a few moments, Albert and Jane came downstairs. Albert directed Jane to sit down in the chair where he had been sitting. Cora put her knitting needles on the table and reached over to take Jane's hand. Albert took a deep breath, slowly opened the letter and began to read. His eyes went wide, and he started to smile. "He's alive! He's alive! cried Albert.

Cora and Jane looked at each other in disbelief. This was not the news they were expecting to receive. Albert started to read the letter:

"We wish to inform you that your husband, Lieutenant John Lewis, is alive and in a prisoner of war camp in Germany. We were notified after the sinking of his ship, that he was picked up by an Italian patrol boat and captured. We have received word from the Red Cross that John is doing well and has no serious injuries."

Albert did not read any more and looked at the women and smiled. "He's alive...I can't believe he's alive." The women got up from their chairs, embraced each other and began to cry. Albert then went over to the women and put his arms around them both.

CHAPTER 10

Albert Lewis was sitting behind the oak desk in his office at the Harbour Breton Hospital. As he was preparing to finish up for the day and head home, the door to his office suddenly opened. A nurse stuck her head inside the door and excitedly said, "It's over...the war is over! The Germans have finally surrendered. They just announced it on the radio!"

Albert slammed his hand on his desk and said, "Finally! Thank God it's finally over."

Albert had been expecting this news for the past week or so. He had hoped that after the success of the D- day invasion, the war would have ended a year ago. Albert, like most people, had not expected the war to go on for as long as it had after the invasion. At least it was over now, he thought to himself. Albert knew this meant that his son John would be able to return home soon. They had received very limited information about John over the past few years. All they really knew was that he was still alive and somewhere in Germany. Several prison camps had been liberated already but since they had not received any news, they guessed that the camp where John was located must have been deep inside Germany.

Albert jumped up from his chair, grabbed his coat and hat and headed out the door of his office. He stopped and told the nurse that he was heading home and if they needed him, they could send someone to get him. I want to get home and give the good news to Cora and Jane before they hear it from anyone else, he thought to himself.

Bill walked out of his garden and closed the gate behind him. He had just finished his dinner and was going to head back down aboard the schooner. Preparations for the new summer fishing season had started today. Bill was happy to be getting back to work after the long winter. The fishing had been good these past couple of years and Bill hoped they would have success again this year. As Bill walked out onto the dirt path that was used as the main road, he saw Albert walking quickly, almost running toward him. Bill waited for Albert to get closer and then he asked, "Is everything ok, Albert b'y?"

"Yes, Bill. Did you hear the news? The war is over in Europe. They just announced it on the radio," said Albert as he did not even break his stride and continued to briskly walk past Bill.

"That's good news. I better go tell Martha," replied Bill.

"Yes, Bill I have to get home and tell Jane and Cora. Hopefully, this will mean that John will be home soon," replied Albert as he continued on his way.

Bill opened the gate and went into his garden. He then walked quickly back into the house to give Martha the good news. This news also meant that Angie would finish her service and hopefully be discharged soon. Angie and Hal would be starting their lives together now and moving to the United States. Bill and Martha's son, Leo, had just signed up for the Canadian Army so Bill knew that Martha would be happy to hear that the war was now over. Both Lawrence and Bill Jr. also had plans to enlist in the merchant navy this year as well. Now that the war was over the boys would probably just want to keep fishing with their father - he hoped so anyway. Bill opened the door to go inside and give his wife the good news.

Albert threw open the kitchen door of his house and startled Cora and Jane who were sitting at the kitchen table. John Jr., who was almost five years old now, was sitting on the floor playing with a toy sailboat.

"Have you heard the news?" asked Albert.

Both women looked surprised and said nothing for a few moments. Then Cora asked, "What news? What are you talking about?"

"It's over…the war is over…the Germans have surrendered," replied Albert. He then picked his grandson up off the floor and lifted him high in the air. "Your daddy should be home soon, my boy…you'll finally get to meet your daddy," said Albert as he gave the boy a hug.

It was a beautiful spring day. The wharf in Harbour Breton was crowded with the people of the community who were eagerly awaiting the arrival of the coastal boat. Albert, Cora, Jane and John Jr. were standing on the wharf along with almost everyone else in the community. This was the day they had all been so eagerly waiting for these past five years. John would be on this boat. He had arrived in St. John's a few days ago along with the first of the Newfoundland troops that had returned home from overseas. Albert's excitement prevented him from eating that morning.

Bill and Martha were also waiting on the dock, but this day would be a sad one for them. Bill and Martha were standing on the dock with Angie and Hal. The young couple had both received their discharge papers and they had just spent the last two weeks in Harbour Breton. They would be traveling to St. John's to take the train to Port aux Basque. Then they would be off to Halifax where they had passage booked on a ship to Boston. From there they would travel to Hal's hometown of Albany, New York, so Angie could finally meet his family. The young couple would be getting married in a month or so and then move to Camden, South Carolina, where Hal would be starting a new job. Angie and Hal had wanted Bill and Martha to travel with them so they could attend the wedding, but they could not as Bill would be fishing. Bill was grateful that he had been in port these past few days and he had been able to see Angie and Hal. He had been worried that he was not going to see them at all before they left for the United States.

The coastal boat pulled alongside the dock. The lines were sent ashore and the gangway was put out. Several young men in uniform made their way down the gangway onto the dock to meet their families who were eagerly awaiting their arrival. Then, there were several other people that disembarked. Albert looked on but was starting to get worried as he did not see John yet.

"Where is he? I can't see him," said Cora.

"I hope he didn't miss the boat," sobbed Jane.

 John appeared at the top of the gangway.

"There he is, I see him!" said Cora as tears filled her eyes.

John slowly made his way down the gangway with the help of one of the crewmen of the coastal boat. When they stepped onto the dock, the crewman handed John a cane and then the men shook hands. John was wearing his Royal Navy uniform. He placed the cane into his right hand and with the aid of the cane, slowly made his way along the dock. Albert, Jane and Cora made their way over to greet John. He saw them and smiled. They all stood for a moment just looking at each other. Jane then went over to her husband, wrapped her arms around him and began to cry. John looked toward his mother and father. Cora's eyes were full of tears, too.

"Well, I'm home. Not the man I was when I left, though...I'm afraid it's been a hard-few years," laughed John.

"I don't care...I'm just so happy you're back," cried Jane.

When Jane stepped away, Cora walked over to her son and hugged him tightly. John looked toward his father and reached out his hand, but Albert did what his father, John Lewis, had done so many years ago when Albert had returned from the first world war - he put out his arms and gave his son a hug. John Jr. was hanging onto his mother's leg. He was not sure who this strange man was and what all the fuss was about. John looked down at his son. Other than the picture that he carried with him, it was the first time he had laid eyes on his little boy. Tears started to stream down his face as he put his hand on the little boy's head. The little boy shyly looked away and buried his head in his mother's leg.

"Come on, let's get home. We all have a lot of catching up to do," said Albert.

Bill and Martha were standing at the bottom of the gangway with Hal and Angie. Bill shook Hal's hand, then Hal headed up the gangway and aboard the boat. Angie and Martha had tears in their eyes now. Angie went to her mother, hugged her and said, "I'll write you as soon as we get to the states." She then went to her father and gave him a hug and a kiss. Then she turned and made her way up the gangway to join Hal who was waiting for her. Angie was the last passenger to board the boat and as soon as she was aboard, the gangway was pulled in and the lines were let go. The engines came to life as the coastal boat made its way off the dock and headed out into Fortune Bay. Bill put his arm around his wife and said, "Come on, old woman, lets get home to check on them boys of ours...they probably got each other killed by now." Martha laughed as they both started to make their way home.

◆ ◆ ◆

John was sitting in the waiting room of the hospital. There were several other people waiting to see the doctor today. Three of the other men waiting, were war veterans that had been disabled due to injuries received during the war. John and these men all knew each other and were about the same age. John still had to use his cane and would have to do so for the rest of his life because of a beating he had taken during his years in the prisoner of war camp. One of the other young men had a leg missing. He had served with the 59th Newfoundland Field Regiment and had been wounded during the battle of the Bulge. Another young man lost a hand in an accident while working as a logger in Scotland. The fourth veteran in the room was blind. He had lost his sight during a U-boat attack on a merchant vessel that he had been serving on in the North Atlantic. He was sitting in a chair between his elderly mother and father.

The nurse called a name and the blind man stood up and with the help of the nurse, made his way into Dr. Albert Lewis's office. The nurse helped the man over to a chair where he sat down.

"Just give me a call when you're done and I'll help you out to your mother and father," said the nurse as she left the office and closed the door behind her.

"Well, Peter, how are things going? What can I do for you?" asked Albert.

"It's the headaches, Doctor, they're getting worse. I can't sleep. Between the nightmares and the headaches, I don't sleep too much," replied the young man.

"Have you been taking the pills that I gave you?" asked Albert.

"Yes, Doctor, they was working but they're gone and I can't get anymore. I don't have any money,"

"Have you received your war pension check yet?" asked Albert.

"They say that I don't get one, Doctor."

"What do you mean, you don't get one?" asked Albert.

"No, Doctor, they said its only fer men that served in the military. Us men that served on the merchant ships or cutting wood, don't get anything."

"That can't be right," said Albert

"I got a letter in the mail yesterday. I had to get the priest to read it...my poor mother and father can't read. I don't know what in the name of God I'm supposed to do. Poor Mom and Daddy don't have anything - just the bit of money they get from my brothers and sisters. They all got families of their own...they can't keep me. It would have been better if I went to the bottom with the ship I was on. I'm no good to anyone anymore...I'm just a burden on my family now."

Albert got up from his chair and went over to examine the young man. He then went over to the door and told the nurse to come inside. Albert said something to her quietly, then she left the room and came back in after a few moments with a glass bottle that had some pills inside. The nurse handed Albert the pills. He took them from her and said, "Tell Peter's mother and father to come in." The elderly couple entered the room and walked over to where their son was sitting. Albert handed the bottle of pills to the young man's father.

"We don't have any money for them pills yet, Doctor. I'll get a bit of money from me daughter next week," said the young man's father.

"Don't you worry about that - pay when you can and make sure you don't go without. Come back and see me whenever you run out," said Albert.

"Thank you, Doctor Lewis," said the young man, as he got up from the chair with the help of his father and mother and headed out of the room.

Albert went back to his chair. He was furious. It all must be some sort of mistake, he said to himself. He would have to look into it after he had seen his patients for the day. The door opened again and the young man who was missing his leg came into the room with the aid of crutches.

"Well, Jack, how are you today?" asked Albert.

"Good, Doctor. I'm here to get the measurements taken fer me wooden leg. I got a letter yesterday with my pension check saying that I needed to get a doctor to fill out this paper with the measurements and send it in. They're going to send me a letter and I'll have to go to St. John's to get me wooden leg," replied the man.

"You got your pension check, did you?" asked Albert.

"Yes, Doctor. I don't know what I would have done without that. I can't fish any more with only one leg," replied the young man.

Albert opened the letter and proceeded to take the measurements that were required to fill out the form. After several minutes Albert put the form back in the envelope and handed it back to the young man.

"Thank you, Doctor," said the young man.

Albert went over to Jack and helped him up from his chair. The man put a crutch under each arm and headed out of the room. A few seconds after he left, the young man who was missing a hand, came into the room and sat down.

"Good day, Mike, what can I do for you?" asked Albert.

"I would like to get a cover fer where me hand use to be. I got a letter back from the government yesterday saying that I won't be getting a pension. I have to try and work. I'll have to go inshore fishing with my brothers," said Mike.

"You can't get a pension either?" asked Albert.

"No Doctor, they said it was only for people that served in the military. If I knew that, I would have stayed the hell home and fished with me brothers... I'm sorry for cursing, Doctor."

"Don't worry about that, my boy, you have got a right to swear. This can't be right. You men that served in the forestry units and on the merchant ships have just as much right to a pension as anyone else. Someone in the government will come to their senses soon. I'll order a wooden hand for you. In the meantime, if you start fishing, just make sure it's well covered so you don't injure your arm.

"Thank you, Doctor,"

"Your welcome, Mike. I'll let you know when your hand arrives."

The young man got up from his chair and headed out the door. After a few seconds, John walked into the room. He went over to the chair and sat down.

"John, you don't have to come up here - I can examine you at home," said Albert.

"That's ok, Father, it's good to get the exercise. I was hoping this leg of mine would start to get better and I wouldn't need this bloody cane anymore," said John.

"Just keep getting some exercise and it should start getting a bit easier for you to walk," said Albert.

'There's something else that I have to talk with you about. I haven't been able to sleep and when I do, I wake up in the night kicking and screaming. I guess I'm still trying to fight those dam Nazi guards. Jane doesn't say anything, but I know it scares her."

"I'm afraid it may be some time before that changes, John. I had bad dreams for many years after the war - I still get them from time to time. I think we'll take the memories from our war years to the grave with us. The more time you spend with Jane and Johnny, it will help to put those dreams to the back of your mind. I can give you something to help you sleep, if you want."

"I'll give it some more time. I don't need another crutch along with this one," Albert said as he lifted up his cane.

"Well, I got my first check today in the mail. At least I'll be able to help you and mother with our keep. I don't want us to be a burden to you and mother. We'll start looking for a place of our own soon, anyway," said John.

"Now, I don't want to hear any of that talk. Me and your mother have lots of room in that house. I don't imagine your sisters will be back here to live anymore. They'll be finished their schooling next year and I'm sure they'll be taking up teaching positions in St. John's. They both have a taste for the city life now, so they won't be back here."

"You may not say that when I tell you that our family will be getting a bit bigger," laughed John.

"Yes, I know that Jane's mother is getting up in age and is finding it hard to take care of herself. She's welcome to live with us. She can sleep in Jane's old room downstairs. Then she doesn't have to worry about climbing up and down those stairs," said Albert.

"There'll be one more addition to the family, too," said John.

"Well, now, that's wonderful news," said Albert as he went over to shake his son's hand. "Another grandchild...that's wonderful!"

"You may change your mind when you have two youngsters running around the house now that you and mother are getting older. You and mom may want your peace and quiet," said John.

"I don't want to hear anymore of that talk. You can all return the favor when me and your mother get too old to get around anymore," laughed Albert.

"Come son, let's get home. We're both lucky men to have survived what we did during those war years. We were able to get home and meet two loving women and have children of our own. I'm sure that you, like me, have known many men that didn't have a chance to live long enough to do those things. Let's get home. I wonder what's for supper."

Both men laughed as Albert went over to get his coat and hat off the rack. John picked up his cane and walked out of the room. Albert put his coat over his arm and put his hat on his head. As he left the room, Albert smiled and closed the door behind him.

THE END

ABOUT THE AUTHOR

Brian Johnston

Brian Johnston was born and raised in Harbour Breton, Newfoundland, and currently resides in Saint John, New Brunswick, with his wife and son. He has made his living at sea for the past 30 years as a cook. Generations of his family have made their living on the sea.

BOOKS BY THIS AUTHOR

A Fortune Bay Fisherman's Tale

A Dark Spring

12765650R00077